Praise for *God Bless Us Every One*

"*God Bless Us Every One* is a delightful holiday novella that is sure to put you in the Christmas spirit. Eva Marie Everson brings her characters to life and tugs at your heartstrings with a sweet romance and a message of family forgiveness. Quotes from Dickens's *Christmas Carol* give added depth and meaning to the story. Grab a cup of cocoa and enjoy this story!"

—**Carrie Turansky**, author of *A Refuge at Highland Hall* and *Shine Like the Dawn*

"What combination is better than this? Eva Marie Everson and Christmas! *God Bless Us Every One* has all the qualities that make her so special as a writer: characters that connect with readers, a heart-touching storyline, and crisp dialogue . . . all of which keeps us turning the pages until the very end. Everson had me at Merry Christmas."

—**Sandra D. Bricker**, author of Live-Out-Loud fiction, including the Another Emma Rae Creation series and the Jessie Stanton series for Abingdon Press

"Everson has penned a sweet holiday tale spiked with plenty of peppermint! What better framework for redemption than a community production of *A Christmas Carol*? Throw in a wayward father making amends and an old high-school crush and you have a surefire recipe for discovering the true meaning of Christmas. Everson delivers forgiveness, renewal, and pure joy as sweet and satisfying as a mug of hot chocolate with marshmallows."

—**Sarah Loudin Thomas**

A Contemporary Christmas Carol

GOD BLESS US EVERY ONE

EVA MARIE EVERSON

Abingdon Press
Nashville

God Bless Us Every One

Macro Editor: Ramona Richards

Published in association with Wheelhouse Literary Agency

Library of Congress Cataloging-in-Publication Data

Names: Everson, Eva Marie, author.
Title: God bless us every one : a contemporary Christmas carol / Eva Marie Everson.
Description: First edition. | Nashville, Tennessee : Abingdon Press, [2016]
Identifiers: LCCN 2016012082| ISBN 9781501822698 (paperback) | ISBN 9781501822704
   (e-book)
Subjects: LCSH: Christmas stories. | GSAFD: Christian fiction.
Classification: LCC PS3605.V47 G63 2016 | DDC 813/.6—dc23
LC record available at https://lccn.loc.gov/2016012082

Epigraphs taken from Charles Dickens, *A Christmas Carol in Prose Being a Ghost Story of
Christmas* (London: Chapman & Hall, 1843).

16 17 18 19 20 21 22 23 24—10 9 8 7 6 5 4 3 2 1
MANUFACTURED IN THE UNITED STATES OF AMERICA

In memory of Rachel LouAnn Richards,
who lived well and brought much joy,
who loved with her whole heart
outshining the stars in the sky.

1

—◦◦◦—

"Bah! Humbug! Merry Christmas! What right
have you to be merry? What reason have you to be
merry…in such a world of fools as this? What's
Christmas time to you but a time for paying bills
without money; a time for finding yourself a year
older, but not an hour richer?"

—*Ebenezer Scrooge*

She couldn't believe it. She absolutely could *not* believe it.

Yet here she was, not a week before Thanksgiving. Five weeks before Christmas.

How would she tell Sis? Never mind *how*. *What* would she tell Sis?

Charlie Dixon—the newly *unemployed* Charlie Dixon—slid her iPhone across the top of her desk toward herself. Pushed it back. Picked it up, juggling it like one of those stress balls she wished she had right about now. Then, taking a deep breath, she pressed the Home button with her thumb and entered her passcode.

The screen displayed a photograph of her and Sis shivering in the New York City cold during their last visit there, grinning like girls, the Rockefeller Center Christmas tree lit up behind them. She smiled, then grimaced at the older woman's face, surrounded by a faux-fur hood and pressed close to her own. Sixty-four with nary a wrinkle.

Okay. Maybe one or two. But few would guess that Sis wasn't a sibling at all, but her grandmother. Most folks thought them to be mother and daughter.

"May as well be," Charlie breathed out.

She entered the code for her grandmother's number and waited.

Sis opened the conversation without so much as a greeting. "If you're calling to tell me you can't make it next week, don't."

Charlie forced a smile. "No, Sis. I'll be there. I, uh..." She looked up at the ceiling, dotted with amber watermarks. Nothing unusual for Florida ceilings, especially in buildings as old as this one. "I, uh...was thinking...maybe I'd come a few days early."

"Why?"

"Why?" Charlie coughed out a chuckle. "Why *not*? Can't a granddaughter come see her grandmother without twenty questions?"

"Mm-hmm. I don't remember asking twenty questions."

Charlie's shoulders dropped a good two inches. She picked up a lone paper clip and twirled it between her fingers. "Sis, I've got some time off." *A lot of time off to be exact.* "I've got some time off and—"

"When will you be here?"

She released her pent-up emotions with a long sigh. "Saturday?"

That gave her the rest of the day to pack up her office, return to her apartment, and figure out what she'd do now that—

"I've got a meeting with the high school drama teacher on Saturday."

Charlie smiled weakly. "You're *really* taking on the Christmas play again this year?"

"I am," Sis returned quickly, her words determined.

"Even after last year's debacle?"

"Last year we didn't have..." Sis's voice trailed off as though something beyond the conversation had stolen her attention.

"Didn't have what?"

"Uh, this year our proceeds are going to a homeless shelter. What do you say to that?"

"That's…that's nice, I guess." Just like Sis to come up with something so heartfelt. "What inspired that?"

"Well, there's something—someone…" Sis's voice trailed. "How about if we talk about it when you get here?"

Charlie glanced at the wall clock across the room. She had less than fifteen minutes to pack up and get out. "That's probably for the best. I've got an appointment in a few so, I'll…what time is your meeting on Saturday?"

"Three."

Testament, North Carolina, was a good eight hours by car. Nine to nine and a half if she stopped her usual half dozen times. If she left at her typical departure time—five in the morning—she'd arrive by two. "I should be there already, but I'll be tired." In other words, don't ask me to be a part of this.

"Of course you will. Call before you leave."

Charlie nodded as though her grandmother could see the action. "I will."

"Love you more than blueberry pie."

Tears formed at the words, an old exchange between the two of them. "Love *you* more than peach cobbler," she returned.

Charlie ended the call, stood, and looked around her. There really wasn't that much to gather—a few framed photographs, a silk plant spilling its leaves down a laminate shelf, some books, a stuffed black bear she'd been given by one of the students here at Miss Fisher's School for Girls, one of the ten most exclusive private schools in the nation, located in the heart of Florida's equestrian farmland.

She turned and peered through the open plantation-style slats of the window blinds at the rolling green grass of the outer complex, then beyond to where about a half dozen horses grazed. Class was in session, so no one milled about other than the occasional employee, mostly those who worked with the horses.

Charlie glanced at her watch and sighed. Ten minutes. She needed to hurry. She grabbed the cardboard box sitting empty by her desk. Her stomach tightened, remembering the look on Clara Pressley's face as she shoved the box into Charlie's hands not an hour ago. "Pack your things, Miss Dixon," she said, her face pinched. "With your latest shenanigans, your days at Miss Fisher's have come to a close."

Shenanigans.

If only she'd had a minute to explain her actions, perhaps Mrs. Pressley wouldn't—no, who was she kidding? Mrs. Pressley had taken an immediate dislike to her the moment she'd taken the role of headmistress six months earlier. Even then, Charlie had seen the writing on the old proverbial wall. She and Clara Pressley were cut from two very different cloths.

"At least I'm not stuck in the 1800s," Charlie muttered as she placed a short stack of her personal books—mostly collections of modern plays—at the far left corner of the box.

"What are you doing?"

Charlie's body jerked at the words coming from her open office door. She placed a hand on her chest. "Marjorie…"

Marjorie Phelps, French II teacher by day and Charlie's best friend and roommate, stood just inside the office.

"Nooo," Marjorie breathed, walking to where Charlie stood. "Tell me she didn't do it, *s'il vous plaît.*"

Charlie reached for the manila envelope stuffed with her severance details, most of which she hadn't read. "*Oui.* She did it. And all because of the musical I chose for the Christmas pageant."

"And right here at Thanksgiving…" The petite blonde crossed her arms and frowned. "You'd think she could have waited until after Christmas." She reached for the framed photo of the two of them taken at Ocala's last celebration of the Kentucky Derby from the bookcase and slapped the stand flat against its back. "What are you going to do?"

The thick brunette braid Charlie typically wore had worked its way over her shoulder. She slung it back. "I'll start with this office. I only have a few minutes to clear out of here before security comes." She glanced at her office desktop computer. "My passwords have already been changed by IT, so I can't even get into my files or e-mail my students."

"But you're friends with many of them on Facebook, right?"

"Facebook, Twitter, Instagram, Snapchat." She raised her brow as Marjorie continued with the packing. "All that social media stuff Mrs. Pressley thinks is the devil's workshop."

Marjorie shook her head, stopping Charlie from going on before the walls took names. "We'll talk about it later. How long do you get to stay in our apartment?"

"Until the end of the week."

"*What?*" Marjorie nearly dropped the potted silk plant.

"Careful there," Charlie said, reaching for it. "I'm going to Sis's on Saturday." She shrugged. "And I'll figure it out from there."

Tears formed in Marjorie's eyes, God bless her. "Does she know?"

Charlie shook her head. "No. And if I can help it, she won't."

Marjorie stole a look at her watch. "I gotta go…five minutes 'til the bell." Which meant five minutes until security arrived. "I actually…I just wanted to see if…well, it doesn't matter." She wrapped Charlie in a quick hug. "I'll see you back at the apartment."

Charlie grabbed the stuffed bear as Marjorie reached the door and glanced back at her. "You'll be okay?"

"I'll be fine," Charlie said, though she wasn't sure how truthful the words were. She placed the stuffed bear at the top of the box. "We never know what the day will bring," she said. The words rang with such rhetorical truth she nearly laughed out loud.

Marjorie smiled. "But as Sis always says, whatever the day brings never shocks God."

Charlie pointed at her. "That's right." She forced another smile. "See ya tonight."

Marjorie slapped the doorjamb. "*À plus tard.* Later."

2

―❧―

"Good Heaven! I was bred in this place. I was a boy
here!...There's the Parrot! Green body and yellow
tail, with a thing like a lettuce growing out of the
top of his head; there he is! Poor Robin Crusoe, he
called him, when he came home again after sailing
round the island. There goes Friday, running for his
life to the little creek! Halloa! Hoop! Halloo!"

—*Ebenezer Scrooge*

Little about her hometown of Testament had changed.

Well, maybe a few things, but not enough to truly note. The minute Charlie crossed the city limits—several miles from the actual heart of town—a strange mixture of yester-year and today worked her like a tonic. And not necessarily in a good way.

She drove the familiar streets, her eyes darting, looking for a face she might recognize in the outskirts. Seeing none, Charlie frowned. She hadn't been gone *that* long, had she? Nine years since high school graduation hardly resembled a lifetime. Not to mention that she visited periodically. All the major holidays. A week during the summer.

Okay, so even then she rarely fraternized with the locals. Only with Sis, who hauled her from pillar to post, showing her off like some prize pig. Naturally, on those outings—to places like the Testament Drug Company for lunch in the side café—she saw a few of her old friends now all grown up. She'd gone to school with them from fifth grade to senior year. A few had children of their own now.

Fifth grade…

Charlie gripped the steering wheel of her Hyundai Elantra at the thought of that first year at Testament Elementary. She'd been so afraid back then. What if the other children knew the truth about her? That her parents were convicted felons. That they were serving ten to fifteen in Georgia state prisons. That her father, the man she hoped never to lay eyes on again, was a drug dealer. A liar. Who'd chosen drugs over his own child.

Sis had told her not to worry. "You know and I know," she'd whispered to her that first night, adding a peck to Charlie's mop of dark hair. "And the good Lord knows. I can't think of another soul who *needs* to know."

Later, when asked by a neighbor, "Where's her daddy and mama?" Sis rolled a version of the truth off her tongue as if she'd been practicing for days. "Their business," she'd said with a nod, "has taken them away from little Charlie for a while. Her daddy and I agreed it best for her to come live with me for the time being."

"A while" had turned into five years. By then her parents had managed to commute their sentences for good behavior. *Exemplary*, her father's attorney's letter explained, the one Charlie had sneaked into Sis's desk drawer to read. Exemplary to the state, perhaps, but Sis was having nothing to do with it.

"You listen to me good," she'd said to her son during a phone conversation one evening when Sis thought Charlie to be asleep in bed. "I don't care if you were holding Bible study on Wednesdays and preaching church on Sundays. You come here and try to take this child from my home, and you'll have me to deal with. I don't care if you *are* her father. You're *my* son, and you're not too big for me to remind you of that every once in a while. No, John Dixon, your daughter—whose name is Charlie, by the way, and not 'my kid' as you keep referring to her—*Charlie* is a junior in high school. She's a straight-A student. She's popular with the others, a favorite among the teachers, and active in her church youth program." Sis took a short breath. "Now if you love her as much as you *say* you do, you'll do right by her and leave her be until she's old enough to decide for herself."

Sis had gotten through to him. Good thing, too. By the time Charlie graduated from high school, her mother had run off with another man, leaving no forwarding address, and her father had returned to his "three hots and a cot," as Sis called it. Good riddance to bad rubbish. Forever, she hoped.

Still, no one in Testament was the wiser. To this day, Charlie hadn't bothered to contact her father, and he'd not bothered to contact her. Just as well. She knew her bitterness wasn't healthy, but it ran deep—and with good reason! "Keep the past where the past goes," she said aloud as the Hyundai rolled past the elementary school to a stop sign. She glanced over, noting the new paint trimming the red brick structure. The wooden cutouts of the early Pilgrims. The ones with holes for faces, perfect for photo ops, obviously left over from the week's preholiday festivities.

She'd spent only a year at this school, and still the memories thumped at her heart. The initial dread of anyone knowing the truth about her had soon been overshadowed by making new friends, going to slumber parties, participating in school sports—track, mainly—and having her first and only crush, Dusty Kennedy, the cutest boy in fifth grade. The cutest boy in the entire school all the way to high school graduation.

As her car rolled on toward town, Charlie wondered what he looked like now. She'd not seen him since senior year, and she imagined him balding or, at the very least, with a receding hairline. Perhaps even a rounding gut where once there'd dwelled a six-pack.

She laughed out loud. Maybe that was just wishful thinking on her part. After all, they hadn't even hit thirty yet.

Charlie drove past the Decker Ranch, craning her neck to find the winding driveway. Old habits die hard, she supposed. She'd practically grown up hanging out there. A little farther up the road, the Matthews' property stretched on the right side. She was almost home.

Home. Whatever that meant these days.

She turned the wheel, and the car bumped its way up the narrow stretch of weed-strewn road leading to Sis's nautical-styled cottage nestled beneath a canopy of fall leaves a hundred yards or so from the old barn Sis had never used but declared she'd never tear down. "Gives this property character, don't you think?" she'd say anytime someone suggested demolishing it.

Just like Sis, holding on to the past.

Charlie smiled as she stopped the car no more than a foot from the Nantucket star railing wrapped around the front porch. She looked at the dashboard clock before shutting off the engine. She'd made it before two.

When she exited the car, the screech of the weather vane pulled her gaze upward. Just as quickly, the slamming of the screen door—the one leading to the screened-in side porch—stole her attention.

"There you are," Sis said, leaping over the two wooden steps bookended with clay pots filled with pink-petaled asters.

Charlie laughed as her grandmother wrapped her in a tight hug. The older Dixon drew back, her cornflower-blue eyes made all the more startling by the pure white of her bobbed hair. "Look at you," Charlie said. "How do you do it, Sis? How do you manage to get younger instead of older?"

Sis pushed at Charlie's shoulder. "Who taught you to say things like that, I wonder? Something you learned at that posh school where you're working?"

Charlie's stomach lurched, and she pressed her hand against the flat of it. "Come on, Sis. You look like a magazine ad, all dressed up in that boho skirt and sweater and...are those scrunch boots?"

Sis pointed a toe, turning her foot left to right and back again. "You like? They're hip."

"*Hip?*"

Sis splayed her hands at her waist. "Is that not the right word?"

Charlie answered with a giggle and a shake of her head. "*Hip*'s an okay word, I suppose." She walked to the back of the car, popping the trunk open with her key fob. "You said you have to be at the school at three?" She pulled the larger of her two pieces of luggage from the recesses.

"I do. Want to come, or are you too tired?"

Charlie had to admit she wasn't tired at all. Somehow, even with the stress of losing her job and having a nine-hour trip behind her, she felt reenergized. Probably the change in weather, which in Testament was crisp and scented with burning leaves. A sharp contrast to the humidity that hadn't quite left Ocala, keeping the scent of hay and horses at a premium. "Actually, I'm feeling kinda good right now, Sis."

Sis reached for the smaller piece of luggage now at Charlie's feet. "Then let's get you inside and freshened up a little." She started toward the screen door. "Oh, I know. We'll stop at The Spinning Bean on our way. They have this new pumpkin latte you have to try."

Charlie brought up the rear, dragging her luggage over the still spongy grass. "So what play are y'all doing this year?" she asked, her focus on her sandaled feet. She'd need to pull out warmer shoes before they left.

Sis paused at the top step as she opened the screen door. "*A Christmas Carol*. And I need to talk to you about—"

Charlie stopped and looked up. "You're kidding me, right?"

Sis feigned indignation. "What's *wrong* with *A Christmas Carol*?"

"You mean other than the fact that it's been done to death?" Heavens, but wouldn't Sis give Clara Pressley a run for her money in the "let's keep it old-fashioned" department? How one woman could look so modern and think so old . . .

"Ha. Ha." Sis pulled at the burnished brass door handle and stepped onto the porch, holding the door for Charlie to enter.

"You know, Sis," Charlie said, huffing as she pulled her luggage up. "There are some fantastic current musicals out there. In fact, I was working on one with the girls at Miss Fisher's before I . . . uh . . . before we took our Thanksgiving break." New hope sprang into Charlie. Perhaps all the work she'd done before being fired hadn't been a loss.

"Mm-hmm." Sis ambled down the length of the porch toward the side door. "You'll have to take that up with the new drama teacher." She turned and smiled at Charlie as though she were in on a classified top secret.

Charlie stopped. "New drama teacher? Someone I know, or did the county finally spring for someone outside its traditional circles?"

Sis grinned. "Well, I suppose that's how you look at it. He *is* outside the traditional circles. He's young and just *full* of ideas, and he *is* someone you know."

Charlie tilted her head. "Who?"

Sis smiled again, then pushed the door open. "Dustin Kennedy," she said as she strolled into the house.

3

―∞―

"Merry Christmas! Out upon merry
Christmas!...If I could work my will, every idiot
who goes about with 'Merry Christmas' on his lips,
should be boiled with his own pudding, and buried
with a stake of holly through his heart. He should!"

―*Ebenezer Scrooge*

Dustin Kennedy. *Dusty*.

He had returned to Testament. And not just to visit. Dustin had come to live, apparently, *and* take the role as the new drama teacher.

"So...um..." Charlie asked her grandmother as the older woman's BMW backed out of the parking place in front of The Spinning Bean. "Dusty." She took a sip of the pumpkin latte and felt a rush of autumn flow through her. "Mmm...good."

Sis's coffee rested in the cup holder between them. "Isn't it? And yes, he's back. Your old crush."

Heat that hadn't come from the latte rushed through her. "Sis..."

Sis laughed as she shifted the car to Drive. "No matter how many other boys you dated, you always had your eye on Dustin."

"And whomever *he* might be dating." The words slipped from her lips without warning. She took another sip of coffee in hopes of a cover-up.

"He was a cutie all right. Quite the ladies' man. Still is."

Charlie looked over at Sis. "Still is what? A ladies' man or a...a cutie?"

Sis turned the car right and headed through a residential area of stately homes, all with manicured lawns, some decorated with bales of hay and cutouts of Native Americans and the early settlers. Many of the doors and windows boasted wreaths of burnt orange and red and vibrant yellow leaves. Others had thick pumpkins, a few with faces, lining the front porch steps.

"A cutie," Sis finally answered.

"So . . . what's he up to these days? Besides being the drama teacher for a bunch of hormonal high schoolers."

"You should know what that's about."

Boy, did she ever. Not that Sis needed to know the fine details of her unemployment. "Back to my question."

"Well," Sis began, "he's got the most adorable little boy—"

"He's married then?"

Sis eyed her. "No. He's not."

"Divorced?" Couldn't be. Who in her right mind would divorce Dusty Kennedy?

"No."

Charlie's breath caught in her throat. "His wife *died*?" She whispered the last word.

"Yes." Sis turned the steering wheel, and the car bounded into the high school parking lot. Charlie immediately spied a Jeep Grand Cherokee—new, from the looks of it—complete with vanity plate: DRAMA1.

Charlie pointed. "Dusty's?"

Sis nodded. "But you might want to practice saying *Mr. Kennedy* before we go inside and the students start arriving."

Mr. Kennedy . . . Charlie allowed the name to consume her thoughts. Anything, as long as she didn't have to think about the fact that she was about to see him again face-to-face.

She stepped out of the car. The steam from her coffee met the cooler air, bringing a whiff of pumpkin to her nostrils. She breathed it in. *Mr. Kennedy . . . Mr. Kennedy.*

"Follow me," Sis instructed. Charlie did, taking in the familiar outdoor hallways stretching in front of classrooms.

Three wings made up the high school—T Wing, H Wing, and S Wing—each holding twelve classrooms. Sis ambled along, talking about this and that, none of which Charlie comprehended. Instead, she concentrated on the room numbers. *I took American history in this room . . . art here . . . chemistry there . . .*

"Here we are," Sis said, stopping in front of the old drama classroom. She opened the door and Charlie continued to follow.

"Hey there, Mrs. Dixon."

Charlie heard the voice before she saw the man, the one down on his haunches and peering over his shoulder in the back of a room dominated by shelves haphazardly lined with books. Seeing her, he stood. She gripped her coffee cup to the point of almost squashing the contents.

"Dustin, you remember my granddaughter, don't you?" Sis asked as calmly as if she'd inquired about whether he wanted pie with his coffee. "I believe you two went to school together."

Nice, Sis.

He had already made it halfway to them, hands holding several small playbooks, when he stopped. "Charlie?" His voice went up an octave.

Charlie held up her free hand. "Hi there."

His face—the one that had somehow gotten more handsome, the one with the Scott Eastwood eyes and brows, the one with the pouty lips and chiseled jaw—registered honest pleasure at seeing her. He dropped the books on a nearby desk and, before she could prepare, wrapped her in a warm hug of cotton and denim. "Wow," he said, stepping back. "I didn't expect to see you." He smiled, and she blushed—she was positive she did—before he added, "Are you here for Thanksgiving?"

And Christmas and New Year's..."I am," she replied.

"Charlie teaches at Miss Fisher's School for Girls down in Ocala, Florida," Sis interjected. "Drama."

Dusty took two steps back as though struck by a bullet. "You're kidding." He shook his head. "I don't remember you being in the drama club back in the day."

"I wasn't," Charlie said. "I concentrated more on chorus in those days."

He pointed a finger, wagging it. "I remember that now. Of course, of course." His smile widened. "Miss Fisher's, huh? Sounds classy. Are you here to help us little people with our Christmas play?"

Charlie walked up to the front of the room and placed her cup on the teacher's desk. "I understand you're doing *A Christmas Carol.*"

He picked up the playbooks while Sis took a seat in one of the desks, crossed her legs, and took a long sip of her latte. "We are," he said. He grinned knowingly. "I bet I know what you're thinking...*that old thing?*"

Charlie stared at her feet. "Well..."

"Charlie believes in *contemporary* plays," Sis called to the front of the room.

"I don't *believe* in them, Sis. I simply *prefer* them."

Dusty dropped the playbooks on his desk, adding to an array of papers, pens, and files that Clara Pressley would have demanded he set to rights. "But *A Christmas Carol* is a classic." He raised his hands dramatically. "A *classic*, I tell you." He looked at her again, mischief glinting from his dark eyes. "You don't have anything against Dickens, do you?"

"Not *personally*," she shot back. "I never met the man."

Dusty crossed his arms and rested his hip on the desk. "But I assume you at least appreciate his writings."

Charlie shrugged. "As much as I have to. I teach his works, but I like to allow my students to discuss whether or not he's..." Her words faded.

"He's...?" Dusty prompted.

Sis coughed out a laugh behind her granddaughter. "I believe the word she's looking for is *relevant*."

The Scott Eastwood brows shot together in the middle. "Relevant? Charles Dickens is megarelevant." He reached for one of the playbooks, curled on the edges. "Do you even know the story behind the story?"

Charlie shook her head, trying to remember what she might have learned along the way about the writer and his short work. "It was published in the mid-1800s."

"Eighteen forty-three," Dusty supplied.

New heat rose within her. She swallowed hard, ready to spar with what limited information she had. But before she could, the classroom door jerked open and a flock of teenagers walked in.

4

"But I am sure I have always thought of Christmas
time, when it has come round . . . as a good time;
a kind, forgiving, charitable, pleasant time; the
only time I know of, in the long calendar of the
year, when men and women seem by one consent
to open their shut-up hearts freely, and to think
of people below them as if they really were fel-
low-passengers to the grave, and not another race of
creatures bound on other journeys. And therefore,
uncle, though it has never put a scrap of gold or
silver in my pocket, I believe that it *has* done me
good, and *will* do me good; and I say, God bless it!"

—*Scrooge's nephew*

Sis?" Charlie drew out the name as she placed the last of the washed-and-dried china in the dining room hutch.

"Yes?"

Charlie turned to see her grandmother standing before her with the two crystal goblets they'd used earlier during their quiet Thanksgiving dinner. She took them gingerly and moved to place them in the hutch. "Sis, can I talk to you for a moment?"

Sis's boots clomped across the floor as she left the dining room and headed back into the kitchen. "Is this the part where you tell me you've lost your job and need to move back in with me for a while?"

Charlie's shoulders dropped as she closed the glass doors, sealing the family china and crystal in safety until Christmas. "*How* do you know these things?" She followed Sis to find her folding the drying cloth over a metal hanger near the window.

"Call it a gift."

Charlie narrowed her eyes and crossed her arms. "Want to clarify?"

Sis turned and smiled. "Your friend from school called."

"Marjorie?"

"She was wondering when she should mail your boxes."

Charlie allowed a sigh to escape her lungs. "Fine." She threw up her hands. "So you're on to me."

Sis laughed lightly. "How about we go into the living room and talk about it?" When Charlie didn't answer right away, she added, "I'll light a fire."

Charlie nodded, then dutifully followed her grandmother into the sunken living room. While Sis went to work at the stone fireplace, Charlie sank onto the oversized brown leather loveseat. She grabbed one of the five mismatched throw pillows and wrapped it in her arms as she kicked off her shoes and slid her feet under her.

"I always loved this room," she said, her eyes glancing up to the exposed beams in the ceiling and then over her shoulder to the French doors leading out to a small patio. Darkness had already fallen on the other side, and she could barely make out the wrought-iron patio furniture that would, soon enough, be covered until spring.

The crackling of the newly lit fire drew her attention back to where her grandmother knelt at the hearth. Sis stood, slapped the debris from her palms, and walked to her favorite chair. The old Boston rocker, which had been in the family for three generations, creaked under her slight weight as she eased into it, then pushed back and crossed her legs.

"Marjorie wouldn't spill the beans," Sis said with a tilt of her head. "But she did insist that you would be honest about it all."

Charlie punched at the pillow. "That nasty ole Clara Pressley," she said. "Everything has to be her way."

"The headmistress?"

Charlie nodded.

"Of course it has to be her way, Charlie. She's the headmistress." Sis's hands clasped the ends of the armrests. For the first time, Charlie noted a swelling of her grandmother's joints. Sis wasn't as young as she used to be.

Charlie threw her head against the back of the loveseat. "But she has no imagination," she whined, knowing full well she sounded every bit of five years old.

"In what way?"

"Everything has to be *old*. Old music. Old plays."

"Classic, you mean."

Charlie rolled her eyes with every ounce of the dramatic flair she hoped she'd exude. "You would say that."

Sis didn't respond immediately, but when she finally did, she said, "Sometimes, Charlie, the *old* can be made new again."

"You mean like a revival?"

Sis chuckled. "Something like that." She sighed. "What's next then?"

Charlie collected herself long enough to stare at the fireplace where the flames had grown fat. She repositioned herself to stretch across the length of the loveseat, still cuddling the pillow to her chest. "I'm hoping to stay here until after the first of the year." She pursed her lips. "It's not going to be easy to find another position in the middle of the school year, but I thought I'd go online . . . put out some feelers . . . send in some résumés. I've got enough severance to get me through for a while."

"You know you always have a home here," Sis said, her face brightening in the heat of the fire. "And who knows? Maybe something will come open at the high school here."

Charlie rolled her eyes and laughed. "I can already see where this is going."

———

Sunday morning dawned with the wind whipping around the corner of the house where Charlie snuggled under the warmth and weight of her favorite quilt. Sis had made it for her out of her old tees and jeans and given it to her for her eighteenth birthday. She'd taken it to college but brought it back to cover her childhood bed after she'd declared herself an adult.

Charlie stretched, then rolled over to reach for the cell phone charging on the bedside table. "Seven," she whispered into the chill of the room. Why, now that she was unemployed, she couldn't manage to sleep at least until seven thirty was beyond her.

She climbed out of the antique sleigh bed, threw the covers back over, fluffed her pillow, and then went into the bathroom where she showered, applied the little bit of makeup she wore on special occasions and Sundays, brushed her hair, braided it, and then wrapped herself in a thick terry robe. Moments later, she stepped into the kitchen where Sis stood at the counter, preparing the coffee. She smiled over her shoulder. "Well, good morning, sunshine."

Charlie kissed her grandmother on the cheek. "Backatcha."

"Sleep well?"

Charlie pulled a box of cereal out of the cupboard, then her favorite almond milk from the fridge. "Fabulously. Just not long enough. We're going to church, right?" she asked.

Sis brought two bowls from a cabinet near her head. "It's Sunday, isn't it?"

Charlie nodded her head. "That it is."

"You know..." Sis said, placing the bowls on the table, "Dustin and his son now attend our little church."

Charlie pulled one of the chairs from the table and sat as she fought the grin working its way up from her heart to her lips. "You don't say?"

Dusty Kennedy's son looked more like his father than his father. "The apple didn't fall far from *that* tree," Charlie whispered to Sis as they stepped out of the row at the end of the service.

"You're not going to have a crush on him, too, are you?" Sis teased.

Charlie playfully pinched her grandmother's elbow beneath an oversized thick sweater.

"Charlie!"

Charlie turned toward the sweet voice she'd grown familiar with during her past several visits to Testament. "Ashlynne," she greeted the leggy blonde, who walked alongside her equally tall husband, William Decker. "I hoped I'd see you today."

Ashlynne looped one arm through Will's as the other fell gently over the rise of her belly. "We saw you from the back when we came in."

"Late," Will supplied. He leaned over and kissed Charlie's cheek. "Which is becoming the norm, I'm here to tell you." His head jerked toward his wife, and he smiled.

"Leave her alone," Sis chimed in with chuckle. "She's carrying around a human being in there."

Ashlynne sighed. "Only two more months and then..."

"And then," Sis added, "you'll *really* have an excuse to be late."

Charlie peered beyond William's shoulder to see Dusty walking toward them against the direction of the small crowd of exiting parishioners. She smiled.

He returned it.

Ashlynne and William noticed her gaze and turned. "Dustin," Ashlynne said as William extended his hand, and Dusty took it.

Charlie glanced at the young tyke standing next to his father, hands held together in a protective fist. "Hello," she said. "I'm Charlie, an old friend of your dad."

"Miss Charlie," Dusty interjected quickly.

Charlie smiled as the young boy turned pink, feeling certain her cheeks matched his own. "Miss Charlie," she corrected herself. She looked at the adult faces. "Sometimes I forget where I am."

Dusty cleared his throat. "This is my son," he said. "Jeremy."

"I'm five," the child said.

Charlie sat on an arm of the pew so as to bring herself to an equal eye level with him. "Then I suppose you're in kindergarten."

Jeremy grinned, exposing a gap where a front tooth had once been. "And I like Miss Thornton a lot." Without the tooth, the name came with an emphasis on the *th*, which brought an easy smile to Charlie's face.

"His teacher," Dusty said. He squeezed his son's hand. "We *all* like Miss Thornton, don't we, son?"

Charlie searched her memory for the name. "I don't remember a Miss Thornton, I'm afraid."

"She's new at the school," Sis said. "Like Dustin."

A hint of jealousy tickled the back of Charlie's neck. Was Miss Thornton someone who might have caught Dusty's attention? And, if so, why should she care, really? She wasn't staying long, after all . . . only until—

"I guess you'll be shoving off sometime today," William said suddenly.

Charlie glanced up, then stood. "No, actually. I—"

"Charlie has decided to stay until after Christmas," Sis said.

The crowd in the center aisle of the church had thinned to only two or three. Charlie raised her chin toward it. "I suppose we are free to move about the cabin," she joked.

Their small cluster moved farther into the aisle, then ambled slowly toward the front door. Dusty asked, "What was that funny look about?"

Charlie cut a sideward glance. "What look?"

"When Jeremy mentioned Miss Thornton."

Charlie stopped. "I had a look?"

"Green-eyed. And over a woman who is fifty-five if she's a day."

Charlie opened her mouth to protest, then thought better of it. "And she's new here?" she asked innocently enough.

Dusty laughed in answer. As they continued forward, he added, "I know he's not your type," Dusty said, his attention fully on Charlie, "but if you're going to be here until the first of the year and you want to help with the play . . ."

"Who's not your type?" Ashlynne asked her.

"Dickens."

Will chuckled. "How can Dickens *not* be anyone's type?"

"Hear, hear," Dusty exclaimed over his shoulder.

"Hear, hear," Jeremy parroted.

Dusty stopped and turned. "We're planning to form a Dickensian choir of sorts."

"Of four or—?" Charlie asked.

"Four. Yes."

"Then you won't have a Dickensian choir per se. You'll have Dickens carolers."

Dusty feigned a cough into his fist as he said, "You got me there."

Sis placed her hand on Charlie's shoulder. "What do you think? You're certainly suited for it and—"

"The entire event is for such a good cause," Ashlynne said, her face lighting up. She beamed at her husband, and he smiled back.

"Which is?" Charlie asked.

"The homeless shelter over in Morganton," Dusty answered. "And the indigent here. Your grandmother's idea really."

"But isn't that over in Burke—"

Sis pushed them onward. "If we don't hurry up and leave this church," she stated with authority, "we won't get home in time for supper, much less Sunday dinner."

Charlie frowned at her grandmother. Knowing her as well as she did, Sis's behavior meant she was hiding something. Some reason why she didn't want her granddaughter to know she'd come up with a donation to charity.

And more to the point, why *that* particular charity? And why in Burke County?

5

—❦—

Again the spectre raised a cry, and shook its chain and wrung its shadowy hands.

"You are fettered," said Scrooge, trembling. "Tell me why?"

"I wear the chain I forged in life," replied the Ghost. "I made it link by link, and yard by yard; I girded it on of my own free will, and of my own free will I wore it. Is its pattern strange to *you*?"

Scrooge trembled more and more.

"Or would you know," pursued the Ghost, "the weight and length of the strong coil you bear yourself? It was full as heavy and as long as this, seven Christmas Eves ago. You have laboured on it, since. It is a ponderous chain!"

Charlie helped Sis the following afternoon by bringing all the Christmas ornaments and decorations down from the attic, one vacuum-sealed bin after the other.

"I usually like to wait until closer to the holiday," Sis told her as Charlie placed the final bin on top of a small stack of others, "but with you being here the entire month, I say let's enjoy every last second of it."

Charlie brought her hands to her hips and stretched her back. "I need to leave. I'm meeting Dusty in town at four o'clock."

Sis brightened. "Are you now? When did that happen?"

Charlie winked. "When you weren't looking. Or meddling."

"What do you think about putting the tree over there?" Sis pointed to the French doors as though Charlie hadn't ribbed her.

"Instead of in the corner where we've always put it?"

Sis nodded. "I think I'd like to change things up a bit this year."

Charlie reflected on the earliest Christmas she could recall. "You used to put it there when I was a little girl."

Sis opened the top bin and peered into the collection of carefully wrapped ornaments. "John always liked it there." She smiled wistfully. "He said Santa could see the lights better. Would know how to find him."

Charlie turned to leave the room and the conversation. "Anyway, I'm meeting Dusty in a few to talk about the carolers." She reached for the heavy coat she'd been forced to bring out over the past twenty-four hours and the knitted scarf she'd bought the year before during the post-Christmas sales. "Do you want me to bring you anything from The Spinning Bean?"

"See if they have any of that White Christmas, or whatever it's called," Sis called back to her. "Decaf."

Charlie glanced at her watch. She needed to leave now. "All right then. I'll be back in time for supper."

Charlie rushed from the house and any further thoughts of her father. She understood—more or less—that John Dixon was her grandmother's son. And she surely understood—more or less—that Sis had precious memories of the little boy she'd reared in the very house where they both now resided. Still, that person, that *boy* whose name had found its way to Santa's Nice List, was a stranger to her. She knew him only as the thief. The absent father.

She knew only wearing the shame, even when no one knew the truth.

Charlie blinked back tears as she neared Testament. Overnight, lights had been strung between lampposts where holiday flags now hung. Just yesterday they'd boasted Thanksgiving and autumn leaves. Now holly and wreaths and the silhouette of a crèche.

She reached for her phone to call Sis, to tell her that Christmas had already come to town, and realized the passenger's seat where she usually threw her purse was empty. "Oh, *nooo*," she moaned.

Charlie slowed her car at the next traffic light and turned right, then right again, and again until she headed back in the direction of home.

Within minutes her car bumped along Sis's driveway. Someone had parked a car she didn't recognize in her usual place, right next to Sis's BMW. Charlie frowned at the West Virginia car tag. Who in the world did Sis know from West Virginia?

She parked quickly and jumped out, leaving the car running and her door open before dashing up the steps, along the side porch, and through the front door. "Sis, I—" Charlie stopped, mouth frozen, her words refusing to come.

"Hey," Sis's visitor said softly, even as her grandmother said, "Oh, no."

Charlie could only stare. John Dixon was older, yes, but she would have known him anywhere. In any setting. Especially this one.

His piercing gray-blue eyes met hers as his brow furrowed, adding lines to an already etched face beneath a close-cut beard. His hair, once dark brown, framed his head in shaggy gray.

"Hey," he said again. The scent of recently consumed coffee and a woodsy cologne reached her. "Look at you."

"Charlie—" Sis started.

Charlie raised her hands. "No." She shook her head, keeping her focus on John. "No. I don't believe this." She looked at Sis. "I—I can't *believe* this." She looked over her shoulder to see her purse on the kitchen countertop. "I forgot my—" She didn't bother to finish. Instead, she grabbed it and turned again for the door.

"Charlie, wait," John said, his voice tinged with anxiety. Or was it fear? Certainly not authority. Because surely he didn't think he held any over her.

She swung around, gripping the strap of her handbag. "No," she said. "We have nothing to say to each other."

"I'm sorry," Sis added. "He—he didn't want you to see him like this—he—"

"I saw you leave," he said, taking a step toward her.

Charlie inched back, her breath coming too quickly. She scanned the length of him to further assess time's damage, from the way he wore his jeans—relaxed fit and naturally faded—to the well-fitting denim jacket partially hiding a plaid cotton shirt.

Still the cowboy.

"I waited," he said. "I told Mom—"

Sis wrung her hands as she took a step closer to her son. "Charlie, you only need to listen for a minute, and I'm sure your daddy and I—"

"John!" Charlie shouted, then willed her voice to return to some semblance of normal. "His name is John. He's *not* my . . . my *daddy.*"

"Charlene Anne Dixon," John said, using her full name as if he had the right. "Don't talk to your grandmother—"

She pointed at him. "*Charlie.* Charlie Dixon." Heat rose up inside her and, for a moment, she thought her head might explode. "And the *only* reason I kept my last name is because it also belongs to Sis." Tears stung her eyes. "How *could* you?" She aimed the shaky words at the woman whose own tears had escaped and made watery trails down her cheeks.

Charlie turned, jerked the door open, and nearly stumbled as she ran out.

"What's wrong? I got your text about running late." As soon as he saw her enter, Dusty had stood at the table for two near the back of the restaurant. Sheet music as well as a copy of *A Christmas Carol* lay on the table next to a mug of delicious-smelling coffee while, overhead, the faint chords of "Silent Night" eased through the sound system.

"Nothing," Charlie breathed out, which was something she'd had to force herself to do most of the distance between the cottage and town. "I forgot my purse. I hate being late." She pointed to the seat with a trembling hand. "May I?"

Dusty pulled the chair out for her. "Here you go."

"Thank you." She crumpled into the seat.

Dusty remained standing. "I'll let our server know you're here."

Charlie looked at her watch as he walked away. *Four thirty.*

Within seconds, Dusty returned with a young woman who looked to be no more than twenty. "What can I getcha?" she asked.

"Uh, how about a caramel latte?"

"Size?"

"Medium."

"You got it."

Dusty returned to his seat. "Talk to me," he said softly. "I've been told I'm a pretty good listener."

Charlie shook her head as she shrugged out of her coat. "It's—nothing."

"Hmm." He straightened as Charlie dared to look at him. "What?"

"I'm only hoping you're a better choir director than you are liar."

"Carolers. Four singers do not a choir make."

"Don't try to change the subject," he countered, his eyes never leaving hers.

"I'm doing no such thing."

"Again, I hope you're a better—"

The server returned then with her coffee. "Anything else? We've got some cranberry scones fresh from the oven if I can tempt you."

Dusty smiled up at the young woman. "Bring us two," he said, and she walked away. "With real butter," he called after her.

"It comes with honey butter," she called back.

Charlie's stomach rumbled at the thought.

"Now," Dusty said, drawing her attention back to him. "Talk to me."

"What if I told you it's personal?"

"All God's children got junk," Dusty said. "And I bet I can match you trauma for trauma."

Instinctively, Charlie realized he spoke of his late wife. "So, if I tell you mine, you'll tell me yours?"

He smiled. "Something like that."

She opened her mouth to speak—to tell him he'd have to go first—when two delightfully scented scones were presented. Dusty shoved the papers to one side, then rubbed his hands together. "Go ahead and box another one of these up to go," he said.

"Will do," the server said. "Here's the honey butter." She grinned at them. "It also has a little lemon and orange zest," she said. "You'll think you've died and gone to heaven."

Charlie broke apart her scone and reached for the butter knife resting on her plate. "I could use a little heaven," she muttered.

"Hey there, you two."

She looked up to see Ashlynne and William edging their way around the tables, where only a smattering of customers lingered over coffee and conversation. Ashlynne threw her thumb over her shoulder. "Can you believe they're already putting up the Christmas lights?"

Charlie pointed up. "Listen. I believe that's 'Good King Wenceslas' playing." She glanced at the table. "These scones smell unbearably good. Want to join us?" *And keep me from having to answer any embarrassing questions?*

Ashlynne, who looked as if she'd stepped out of an L. L. Bean catalog dressed in a stretchy cable dress and flat-heeled knee-high boots, and Will, dark and handsome as he'd ever been, shared a look, then nodded. "Do you mind, man?" William removed his trademark cowboy hat as he directed the question to Dusty.

"Of course not. I needed to talk to you anyway." He gathered the papers on the table. "Let's move to a booth."

A minute later, two additional scones had been ordered along with one coffee and a hot tea.

"William is building our sets," Dusty said between bites. "And Ashlynne has agreed to help with costuming."

She grinned from behind the rim of her tea. "It's my *thang*."

"Sounds fun," Charlie said.

Ashlynne laced her fingers around the mug. "Maybe you and I can meet sometime and look at the possibilities together? There's a resale shop that's positively bursting with vintage clothing where I'm sure we can find some things we'll need." She pulled her purse from the back of her chair and dug around until she found her iPhone. "How about Wednesday afternoon?"

"Sure," Charlie said. "I guess."

Dusty leaned over. "Charlie isn't into *vintage*, Ashlynne. She likes *contemporary*." He air quoted the two opposing words.

"That's okay," William said, bringing the final bite of his scone to his mouth. "Once upon a time, Mrs. Decker here wasn't so keen on *country* either. Now look at her." He eyed his wife. "I've loved the city right out of her."

Ashlynne nudged him with her shoulder. "Hush up," she said, then added, "but it's true. There was a time when I wouldn't be caught dead inside a Walmart."

"She didn't even know what a Walmart *was*."

Ashlynne's eyes grew large, even as they winked with merriment. "Hush up right now or you'll sleep with the dogs." Then, turning back to Charlie, she said, "Walmart has the *best* candles."

"I'm fond of their wax cubes myself," Charlie said, then laughed.

Ashlynne took a sip of tea. "So there you have it. I changed my opinion on discount shopping," she said. "Sometimes we simply have to roll with the way things are." She twirled her hand in the air. "Try new things…ideas…" She gave a definitive nod. "I'm living proof that a person can change." Ashlynne glanced at her husband. "Right?"

Will Decker nodded back at her. "Shoot, I reckon."

6

⊶⊷

"How it is that I appear before you in a shape that you can see, I may not tell. I have sat invisible beside you many and many a day."

It was not an agreeable idea. Scrooge shivered, and wiped the perspiration from his brow.

"That is no light part of my penance," pursued the Ghost. "I am here to-night to warn you, that you have yet a chance and hope of escaping my fate. A chance and hope of my procuring, Ebenezer."

A tiny bit of clarity had seeped into Charlie by the time she returned to the cottage—one medium-sized White Christmas Mocha resting in the console cup holder beside her. And even though disappointed that she'd not had any real one-on-one time with Dusty, something about being with Ashlynne and Will had centered her. Helped her see...

As much as she hated to admit it, John Dixon *was* in fact Sis's son. And his words—*"I saw you leave"*—kept rolling around in her mind, helping Charlie realize that a certain level of respect for her feelings had been at play.

Possibly by both John and Sis.

Still, the absence of the car with the West Virginia tag in the driveway came as sweet relief.

And then it dawned on her—the car hadn't been an old clunker as she'd fully expect an ex-convict to drive but a fairly new model. Dark blue. Four doors. A family-style car. Maybe a rental?

She shook her head as she parked, then reached for the peace offering that had filled her car with a faint scent of chocolate.

"Sis?" she called out when she entered through the side door, hoping her voice sounded friendly.

"I'm in here."

Alone? She wanted to ask but didn't. Instead she followed the voice into the family room where Sis had hung a large wreath with white twinkly lights and a large red bow over the mantel, replaced the sofa's everyday pillows with Christmas-themed ones in various sizes, and draped a candy cane quilt over her rocker.

"Sis..."

Her grandmother stood over one of the bins, a strand of cascading evergreen garland stretched between her extended hands. "I thought I'd get started," she said, stepping over the bin and toward the fireplace. "Care to help me hang this?"

Charlie placed the coffee on the low coffee table, then hurried to the far side of the fireplace. "We always do this together," she said. Looking up, she added, "Please tell me you didn't climb on something and hang that wreath all by yourself."

Sis hooked her side of the garland to the end of the mantel, and Charlie did the same. "As if I could." She worked the garland with her fingers, presenting it just so. "Your— my—" She sighed. "John helped." She shrugged. "He hung it. I directed."

Charlie imitated her grandmother's handiwork at the other end, fluffing the previously flattened branches. "Listen, Sis...about that..."

Sis returned to the bin. "You had every right to be shocked. Angry."

"And you have every right to have John here. He's your son. This is your house. I was just—"

Sis pulled two handmade stockings from the bin. "We should have hung these first."

Charlie walked over and took the one stitched with her name. "We can make it work."

"Are we talking about the stockings or our dysfunctional family?"

Charlie walked the stocking to the mantel and slipped the loop under the greenery. "We're not dysfunctional," she mumbled.

Sis guffawed. "What would you call it then?"

Charlie stared at her grandmother, reading the sadness clouding her eyes. Indeed, what *would* she call it? "I brought your coffee," she said, pointing to the coffee table. "But I'm sure it needs to be reheated now."

"Put it in the fridge. I'll heat it up with our dinner." She smiled at Charlie. "I might even share."

Charlie complied, then returned to the living room to find Sis seated in the rocker, the quilt wrapped around her shoulders. "Are you cold?"

"A tad."

"I'll make a fire."

"You know, Charlie," Sis began, "it might help if you ask some questions. Even one or two will help, I think."

Charlie knelt at the hearth and pulled newspaper from the brass bucket where Sis kept old editions and tinder. "Like what?" She looked over her shoulder. "And that doesn't count as a question, just so you know."

Sis smiled.

Charlie twisted the newspaper before placing it on the grate where the ashy remains of last night's fire remained. "I'll clean this out good tomorrow," she said. "So, he lives in West Virginia?"

"No . . . He lives in Morganton."

Charlie's head whipped toward her grandmother. "What?" she barely breathed out.

"Your father is directing the homeless shelter in Burke County."

Charlie couldn't respond. After a silent moment, she turned back to reach for two large logs at the top of the fire-wood rack.

Sis continued. "After his last time in prison, John went into a halfway house up in West Virginia. While he was there, he took a job working at a homeless shelter. The director took a liking to him, treating him more like a son than a criminal. In time, he became the assistant director and then . . ."

Charlie struck a match and lit the newspaper. "Then?" She didn't bother to look at her grandmother. She couldn't.

"There was an opening in Morganton, and he took it."

Charlie sat back on her feet as the flames licked the wood and ate up the paper. "And when did you first hear from him?"

"About six months ago while he was still in West Virginia. We wrote back and forth a few times, then he called. He's . . ."

Charlie folded her hands in her lap. The fire heated her skin, even as her heart grew more impenetrable. *Burn me, but I will not topple. I will not cave.*

She took a deep breath, stood, and walked to the sofa without looking at her grandmother. "He's . . . ?"

"Changed."

"Not by me, he hasn't." She fiddled with a hangnail.

"He's been out of prison for three years, Charlie. He's held an honest job the entire time. He's respected in his work. In three months he's done amazing things with the shelter."

Charlie looked up. "Who are you trying to convince? Me or yourself?"

Sis crossed her arms. "I don't need convincing."

"Well, I do," Charlie answered quietly.

"I understand that. So does he."

Charlie shook her head. "Then why hasn't he bothered to contact *me*?"

"I told him not to. To give you time. I'd planned...I'd planned to talk to you about it while you were here, but then I found out that you'd lost your job, and I thought this might not be the best time."

"Hmm."

"So then I thought we'd talk about it over these next few weeks. Maybe by Christmas."

Charlie's mind worked overtime. *By Christmas?* Memories of sitting around the tree, wrapping paper and bows strung here and there, her father near her while her mother sat curled in an overstuffed chair, her hands wrapped around a steaming cup of cocoa.

Served with marshmallows, like back then...

Before they'd chosen a life of drugs and everything that went with it. Lying. Stealing. Ignoring their only child.

"Does he know anything about my—about Gayle?"

"I asked him once. He said he'd looked her up online. She's no longer in the prison system, if that's any consolation. But he did find a marriage license in her name from a few years back. She married a horse farmer in Kentucky."

Charlie waited, imagining her mother wrangling horses or driving around in a rusty, beat-up truck. When her grandmother said nothing more, she asked, "Is that it?"

"He said he didn't need to know anything else. She knows where you are, and he knows where you are. At least *he's* trying to make his way back, Charlie."

Charlie jumped up from the sofa. "I'm hungry," she said. "What are your thoughts to go with the mocha?"

"Charlie?"

She turned. Her grandmother had stood and was replacing the quilt, just so.

"Do you know why Charles Dickens had such concern for the impoverished?"

Charlie turned. "The era demanded it, I suppose."

Sis looked at her and asked, "But why Dickens? Why the poor? Exactly what was he responding to when he wrote *A Christmas Carol*?"

"I admit I don't know."

Sis smiled then, although it seemed more out of sadness than cheer. "Why don't you find out?"

The words were not really a question but a request. And she knew all too well why Sis wanted her to find out.

But the question remained between them, and Charlie wasn't sure if she was up to knowing the answer.

7

—∞—

"Why do spirits walk the earth, and why do they come to me?"

"It is required of every man," the Ghost returned, "that the spirit within him should walk abroad among his fellowmen, and travel far and wide; and if that spirit goes not forth in life, it is condemned to do so after death. It is doomed to wander through the world—oh, woe is me!—and witness what it cannot share, but might have shared on earth, and turned to happiness!"

On Tuesday afternoon, Charlie stood on the far side of an old Kawai upright piano, flipping through the sheet music Dusty had given her the day before, when the classroom door on the other side of the room opened. She glanced up.

"Brianna," she exclaimed, resting the music against the upper panel. She stepped around the piano, grinning at the young woman she'd known nearly her whole life. "Look at you. You're positively radiant."

Brianna Matthews gave Charlie a quick hug before bringing her fingers up to work on oversized coat buttons. "The weather has dropped out there," she said. "My nose feels frozen."

Charlie fingered the short bob of copper-colored hair. "You cut your hair." She shook her head. "I cannot remember a time when you didn't have hair down to your waist."

Brianna laid her coat over one of the school desks in the high school's music department classroom. "I know. I figured—as a married woman now—it was time."

"How is Rob?"

Brianna blushed. "Amazing. I love him so much, and he's such a good stepdad to Maris." She waved her hands as though erasing one of the old chalkboards in the room. "Not that her father isn't still her *daddy*, mind you. But Rob . . . he's just all-around amazing."

Charlie sighed. Other than her school-days crush on Dusty Kennedy, she'd never been this giddy over anyone—boy or man. For some reason, such an absence in her life stung that afternoon. She turned back to the piano. "Are you in my little quartet?" she asked. "Please say yes."

Brianna followed her to the piano. "Of course. And so are Lisa Hendrix, Perry Jones, and Buddy Hartselle."

"Mister Buddy is singing with us this year?"

Brianna's eyes widened. "Mister Buddy sings with us *every* year. A good old-fashioned Testament Christmas wouldn't be a good old-fashioned Testament Christmas without his baritone."

Charlie held up the pages of music and frowned. "Old-fashioned is the theme of the year, I'm afraid."

"Meaning?"

"Not one contemporary song in all this sheet music."

Brianna leaned over from the back of the piano. "Well...I mean...wouldn't it sound silly to have a Dickens-themed show, complete with four singers in Victorian costume, singing, oh, I don't know... 'Rockin' Around the Christmas Tree'?"

Charlie rolled her eyes. "Thank you, Brenda Lee."

Brianna laughed. "I'm just saying. What *did* Dustin choose?"

Dustin. Charlie wondered if she were the only person on the face of the planet who still thought of him as "Dusty."

"'O Come, O Come, Emmanuel.'" She shuffled the pages as she rattled off the titles. "'The Wassail Song,' 'O Come, All Ye Faithful,' 'I Saw a Maiden,' and of course, 'God Rest Ye Merry, Gentlemen.'"

"Why 'of course'?"

Charlie waved the music in the air. "'God bless you, merry gentleman! May nothing you dismay!'" she declared with an air of drama.

Brianna frowned. "What?"

"It's from *A Christmas Carol*...Scrooge. I believe he was waving a ruler as a weapon at the time, which, by the way, frightened away a *singer.*"

Brianna laughed. "Well, you can't frighten me away with your bad mood."

"Me? I'm not in a bad mood." She plopped down on the piano bench, and it moaned beneath her. "I'm just trying to figure out what's wrong with the Dusty Kennedys and the Clara Pressleys of the world. I mean, what's so awful about adding one or two modern Christmas carols? 'Mary, Did You Know?' or 'Joy Has Dawned'?"

"I don't know that one—the second one—but why don't we sing 'God Rest Ye Merry, Gentlemen' in the arrangement by Barenaked Ladies?"

Charlie brightened. "The one with Sarah McLachlan?"

"One and the same. I have the CD. I can bring it next time if you'd—"

"Hello, hello," a voice boomed as the door opened. "The gang's all here!"

Charlie stood. "Mr. Jones," she said. Then, seeing the others behind him, she greeted them individually. "Get out of your coats," she said lightly. "And we'll get started."

The following day, Charlie kissed Sis goodbye as they walked toward their cars. Both were bundled in coats and scarves, and both carried travel mugs of hot coffee. Steam rose from the tiny openings, emitting the faintest hint of peppermint flavoring. "How long do you think you'll be at rehearsal?" Charlie asked as she pushed a button on her key fob.

"Today's rehearsal will be short and sweet, or at least so Dustin said." Sis opened her car door and grinned back at Charlie. "Shall I send him your love?"

"Sis..." Charlie shook her head. "Really."

Sis laughed. "Have fun with Ashlynne." She started to get in, then stopped. "Are you sure you know where you're going?"

"A Second Chance, right?"

"On Holly Avenue."

Charlie grinned. "Holly—how appropriate."

Sis bent in to place her mug in the cup holder before straightening. "Go all the way to the back. There's a double doorway to the left that will take you into the vintage part of the store. A little pricier, but that's where they put that sort of thing." She paused. "Then again, Missy Adams found an amazing mink coat, circa 1960s, for a song."

"We need muffs and collars," Charlie said, opening her door. "And big hats and..." She climbed into the car, then started it. While she waited for her grandmother to head down the driveway first, she fiddled with the satellite radio in her car until she found holiday tunes.

She sighed at the final measures of Michael Bublé's version of "The Christmas Song" as she backed her car out, then swung around to drive forward. "Merry Christmas to you, too, Mr. Bublé."

"Ah," the DJ crooned as the song faded to silence. "Is that not a wonderful version of an old standard? Now some of you may have been out there in Christmasland declaring your preference for Nat King Cole's version, released in November 1946, which we played last hour. Remember, last hour we played older versions of the Christmas songs we grew up on, and now we're playing the same songs but by contemporary artists." The DJ chuckled. "Here's a little trivia on the song..." Charlie neared the downtown area of Testament, turning right, then left, and heading toward the side street near The Spinning Bean where the consignment shop was located. "…written by Bob Wells and Mel Tormé in the summer of 1945 on, what Tormé later said, was a blistering hot day."

Charlie drew in a deep breath.

Mel Tormé…a memory swept over her…an album cover…the white-haired singer-songwriter sitting in a gold brocade wingback chair before a roaring fire. Behind him, Christmas tree lights twinkled around gold ornaments, and a garland of greenery and fruit swooped from one side of the mantel to the other.

And her mother and father—Gayle and John—wrapped in each other's arms, dancing…gliding, really…to the smooth melody…the violins and the tickling of the ivories…her mother's laughter as she threw back her head…and the way her father nuzzled her throat.

There she sat on the floor by their over-decorated and spicy-scented tree, cross-legged and happy, her new dolly cradled in her arms. And Sis, who always arrived on Christmas Eve, leaning against the doorframe leading to the kitchen, a mug of cocoa wrapped in her hands, beaming at the love between her son and daughter-in-law.

The contentment of her granddaughter.

Until…

Charlie parked the car and swiped at the tears rolling down her cheeks. How could they have given it all up for some silly white powder snorted up their noses? Or dared to or been stupid enough to attempt to transport a stash of it across state lines?

They had ruined everything. Destroyed it all. Their lives, individually and together. They'd shattered Christmas Past.

And now John Dixon wanted her to forgive him.

Well, bah, humbug.

8

—ଛଛ—

"Are you the Spirit, sir, whose coming was foretold to me?" asked Scrooge.

"I am!"

The voice was soft and gentle. Singularly low, as if instead of being so close beside him, it were at a distance.

"Who, and what are you?" Scrooge demanded.

"I am the Ghost of Christmas Past."

"Long Past?" inquired Scrooge: observant of its dwarf-ish stature.

"No. Your past."

Charlie inched her way along the crowded aisles of the warehouse-sized consignment shop, which was overstuffed with secondhand home furnishings, clothes for every member of the family, and shelves stacked with dishes and glassware. Near the back were Christmas decorations. Glass and plastic ornaments; dancing Santas that had, no doubt, done their last hula; and gold-beaded reindeer.

The aisles were filled with shoppers—some who looked as if they had no need of being there and others who appeared to be shopping for Christmas among the castoffs. Charlie cringed. Even as bad as it had been being the daughter of two convicts, life had never required her to open Christmas gifts previously owned by another child.

Thank the good Lord for Sis.

She blinked as an overhead sound system broadcast Josh Groban belting out the first verse of "The First Noel." She glanced up to read a large banner stretched across the back of the store: Thank You for Shopping at A Second Chance...Because Everyone Deserves a Second Chance.

At least he's trying to make his way back, Charlie.

Charlie gripped the edge of a nearby shelf, one stacked with a hodgepodge of well-read paperback books, their spines bent by long creases. Sis's words echoed in her head.

Do you know why Charles Dickens had such concern for the impoverished?

Your father is directing the homeless shelter in Burke County.

She gasped as the inside of her head felt like pink cotton candy wrapped loosely on a paper cone, like the kind John used to buy her at the annual carnival. A wave of dizziness crashed over her. What was happening? Her fingers tightened, squeezing the metal beneath them.

"Charlie?"

She whirled around, inhaling deeply.

John Dixon stood no more than two feet away, concern etched on his face, his brow furrowed. "Charlie, are you all right?"

Now wasn't the time. Not now. Not *here*, surrounded by townsfolk she didn't know. And possibly one or two she did. Charlie straightened, pulled at the scarf wrapped around her neck, and swallowed. "I'm fine. I'm—what are you doing *here*?" She shook her head to push the rapidly spinning thoughts away. "Sis said you worked in Burke County." Her face grew tight, and she felt her lips form a line.

John shoved his hands in the pockets of his black jeans, the ones a shade lighter than the sports jacket he wore over an untucked polo shirt. He shrugged. "I do. I had—" His eyes shot toward the far right back of the store. "I had a meeting with the manager here. We're working on a...a joint project." He offered a weak sort of half smile. "Mom says you're working on the high school play."

"I—" Charlie choked on the rest of her words, not knowing for sure what they would be.

"I guess you know the proceeds are going toward the homeless shelter." He cleared his throat, his eyes studying her. "That's the joint project I'm here about."

Charlie pushed at the wistful tendrils of hair that had escaped her braid as she took a step back. "I can't—I *can-*

not have this conversation with you." She attempted to step around him quickly. Just as suddenly, he grabbed her arm.

"Can't we just *talk?*" he whispered. "A cup of coffee at The—"

"Get your hands off me," she hissed, jerking away.

She dashed through the store, stumbling into a few customers—a mother shaking a rattler at the wailing baby on her hip, a group of teen girls giggling over a rack of denim jackets—all as Perry Como crooned "It's Beginning to Look a Lot Like Christmas" from overhead.

Charlie managed to make it back to the wide, storefront glass doors. She pushed through only to collapse on the other side into Dusty Kennedy's arms. "Charlie," he said, his hands gripping her shoulders. "Are you okay?"

"Get me out of here," she whispered.

He glanced up at the door swinging shut behind her as his arm came protectively around her.

Dusty turned her toward the main street cutting through town. "Come on," he said. "The Spinning Bean is right around the corner."

Charlie stared down at the cinnamon-sprinkled froth floating on the top of her cappuccino. "Thank you," she half whispered as she slipped her iPhone into her purse. "I just sent Ashlynne a text that I might be late."

Dusty leaned over the booth's table, resting his forearms on its edge. Even in her fragile state, she noticed the intensity of his chocolate-brown eyes and the way his brow darted upward in the middle. She was keenly aware of the scent of him—all woods and spice—as the fragrance of his aftershave wafted across the table and the flavor of their coffees.

He was the last person she wanted to talk to about seeing her father.

He was also the first.

"Out with it," he said as his finger grazed the ceramic of his coffee mug. "What's going on with you?"

She attempted a joke. "I thought you were going to share first."

"What?"

Charlie's eyes darted around the room, hoping to avoid his as they took in the holiday decorations that had been hung since they'd been there only days before. She noted the way the light shone on the large glass ornaments clustered in Christmas colors of green, red, gold, and blue, and nestled among boughs of pine-scented evergreens. On the wall overhead, a P. J. Clarke's Christmas-inspired train stretched along a shelf hanging two feet from the ceiling.

She wondered if it worked.

John had always been big on train sets, especially at Christmas. Every year before his incarceration, he'd placed one around the base of the tree. She wondered if the sets were still in the storage bins, if Sis would want to put them out this year, once they got a tree set up in front of the French doors. *John always liked it there.* Sis seemed determined to push her into Christmas Past.

"Charlie?" Dusty's voice brought her back.

She forced a smile as she brought the cappuccino to her lips. "You. Remember? You go first." She took a sip, swallowed, and added, "All God's children got junk?"

Dusty hung his head like an old hound dog. "Yep. We sure do."

"So you tell me first." *And allow me a moment to gather my bearings. To figure out how to tell you that I'm the daughter of convicts.*

His eyes met hers, and he took a deep breath. "You know I was married, right?"

Charlie returned her cup to its saucer as he took a long swallow of his black coffee. "Yeah. Sis said...I mean...you have a son, Jeremy."

Dusty's eyes grew misty and warm. "My boy." He shook his head. "That child has done more to heal my heart than all the balm Jeremiah sought in Gilead."

"Children have a way of doing that." She waited, and when he only stared off, she spoke softly, "What was your wife's name?"

"Emily." His eyes found hers again. "We met in college."

Charlie tried to smile but found it more difficult than she imagined.

"She was...funny and beautiful and caring." He took another sip of coffee, then pushed it out of the way. "And she loved me. Boy, did she love me." Dusty swallowed so hard Charlie heard it across the table and over the sound of "Do You Hear What I Hear?" from the overhead speakers. "After Jeremy was born, Emily had that—you know—that postpartum depression."

Charlie shook her head. "I've heard of it, but I've never...I mean..."

Dusty raised one hand as though he were excusing her, then dropped it. "Of course." He blinked. "Well, the doctor put her on some medication. You know, to help with it all. Then he weaned her off after a while. Only, Emily seemed to get worse instead of better. The doctor admitted her to the hospital—psych ward—and then after a few weeks, she came home."

Charlie reached for her coffee, then decided against it.

"For a few weeks, maybe a month, it seemed like everything would be all right. Then..." His eyes filled with tears.

Instinctively, Charlie reached across the table and slid her hand in his. Dusty's fingers wrapped around the whole of her hand, squeezing. "You don't have to finish," Charlie whispered.

He continued as if he hadn't heard her. "I came home one day. Jeremy was in his crib, screaming his little head off. I called out to Em." He shook his head. "She didn't answer. I gathered Jeremy in my arms—" Dusty brought his free hand up to his heart as though he were cradling a baby. "And I walked into our room. Em was in the bed." One shoulder shrugged. "I thought she was asleep, but then...then I saw the empty medicine bottle on the bedside table. The half-consumed glass of water. Her handwriting scribbled across a piece of paper next to it." A tear slipped from his eye and he sniffled. "I didn't even have to check to know she was gone."

"Oh, *Dusty*." Charlie reached for his other hand, and he readily gave it to her. "I had no idea. If I had..." If she had, what? She'd known his wife had died, but she'd imagined pneumonia or possibly that she'd died in a car accident.

But not by her own hand.

Dusty blew a breath from his lungs as though he'd rid himself of an old demon. "You're the first one in town I've told this to."

Charlie dipped her head to one side. "Not even Sis?"

He gave a light shake of the head. "No. She only knows that Emily died. I guess a woman leaving behind a husband not yet thirty and a baby is enough to cause her to bestow pity."

"How old was Jeremy?"

"Two." He pulled a napkin from the chrome holder and wiped his nose. "Enough about me. Your turn." Dusty raised his brow and nodded.

Charlie straightened, bringing her hands to her lap and lacing her fingers. "I'm not even sure mine is worth mentioning now."

"No, no." Dusty waggled a finger at her. "You're not getting out of it that easily. Come on now. I just totally bared my soul."

"All right," she said quietly, licked her lips, and concentrated on her hands. "I saw my father in A Second Chance."

"Your dad?"

Charlie looked up. "Until two days ago, the last time I saw him, the police were leading him and my mother away in handcuffs."

Dusty fell back against the booth's thick vinyl cushion. "You're kidding, right?"

9

—∞—

"Spirit!" said Scrooge in a broken voice, "remove me from this place."

"I told you these were shadows of the things that have been," said the Ghost. "That they are what they are, do not blame me!"

"Remove me!" Scrooge exclaimed, "I cannot bear it!"

He turned upon the Ghost, and seeing that it looked upon him with a face, in which in some strange way there were fragments of all the faces it had shown him, wrestled with it.

"Leave me! Take me back. Haunt me no longer!"

That's some story," Dusty said several tension-filled minutes later.

"Fortunately," Charlie said around the lump in her throat, "my parents were arrested in Georgia where we lived back then and—social media *not* being what it is today or existing at all for that matter—I could safely come to Testament to live with Sis and no one would be the wiser."

"And you made sure none of us at school ever found out."

Charlie pressed her lips together. "I worked hard to belong. I made good friends. I made good grades. I stayed focused on the present and the future and kept the past where it belonged. In the past."

Dusty pointed to their cold cups of coffee. "Want another cup?"

Charlie shook her head. "I'm sorry I didn't finish this one. The few sips I had were delicious."

"Do you think...? Hmm."

Charlie smiled. "Do I think what?"

"Do you think the reason you have this *aversion* to the classics has anything to do with your desire to keep the past where it—as you say—belongs?"

"I hadn't thought about that." She rested her elbow on the table and her chin on the ball of her fist. "Maybe. Could be."

They sat silent for long moments until Dusty cleared his throat and leaned forward once again. "You have to forgive him, you know."

"Why?"

He cocked a brow. "You know why."

Charlie nodded. "I do. But I—I can't *forget*, Dusty. And I'm not so sure Jesus requires that of us."

"Doesn't He?"

"But *how*? I'm a human being, after all." She paused to see if he would respond. When he didn't, she asked, "Have you forgiven Emily?"

Dusty winced. "Ouch."

"Oh." Remorse rose inside her like bile. "I'm so sorry."

But Dusty's hand came across the table, palm up, as though he wanted her to place hers there.

She did, and the warmth of it eased her regret.

"I'll be honest," he said, "it took a while. Every time Jeremy got sick or did something cute or experienced a milestone . . . I became almost furious with her. Anger is a natural part of the grieving experience—if I heard that once I heard that a thousand times—but in my mind she'd *chosen* to leave us."

"I understand. I've felt that same kind of anger, Dusty. My parents *chose* to end what I remember as being a magical childhood, full of laughter and music and love. They *chose* to start using. To start selling. To start transporting out of Florida."

"They're lucky something much worse didn't happen to them." His brow rose as his hand squeezed. "Or to you." Dusty looked over his shoulder, then nodded toward a wall hanging. "See that sign over there?"

Charlie looked across the room. "Which one? The one about a coffee break or the new one that says 'Merry Christmas'?"

"'Merry Christmas.'"

"Yes." She grinned. "Actually I see them both."

His eyes widened playfully. "Stick with me."

"Yessir."

"Did you know that Dickens—through *A Christmas Carol*—helped coin that phrase?"

"I—no."

"See, before 1843, when he wrote the novella that took him from near bankruptcy to found-again fame, the English had hardly any regard for the holiday." He brought his free hand up and rested two fingers against his temple. "See, the Puritans had all but wiped the celebration off the map. In fact, during the Christmas of 1647, a number of preachers were arrested for attempting to preach on that day."

"Has anyone ever accused you of sounding like a history book?"

Dusty's hand rested on top of hers. Charlie reluctantly placed her free hand on top of the fist formed in the middle of the table. "Stick with me please," he said.

"Okay."

"By the mid-1800s, when the British were beginning to question all this and the first Christmas card was commissioned—so the story goes—Dickens went to Manchester to deliver a speech. While there, he observed the poor . . . the factory workers. And he was stirred. Dickens himself understood what it meant to have much and still be in need. You probably know all this."

"About him and his father?"

Dusty nodded. "You're catching on."

"Where'd you get all this information?"

"Ashlynne." He chuckled. "You know she's the editor in chief of *Hunting Grounds and Garden Parties*. The magazine?"

"Of course. I grew up here, remember. I'm not just some twice-a-year visitor."

"Right, right. Well, she's got the heart of a research hound. As soon as I asked her and William to be a part of the performance, she dug in to learn more about the history. She came to me with the whole story. About how the citizens of England were reexploring Christmas and its traditions, about the first Christmas card being commissioned, and about Dickens wanting to write this story and *believing* in this story so fervently that he was willing to fund it himself."

"I remember studying this in college and thinking...thinking about my parents actually."

"And then?"

She winced. "And then pushing it as far from my mind as possible. After all, it's in the past."

"Maybe you should write a Christmas novella instead."

"Will I become as famous as Dickens?"

"You never know."

They remained silent for a few moments. Charlie breathed out, "Do you think..." then inhaled deeply and exhaled again. "Do you think Dickens ever fully forgave his father?"

"For what? For going to debtors' prison when young Charles was a boy, which landed him in a factory as a worker? Or for continuing to pressure his son for money—not to mention his son's *friends*—once the boy became a man?"

Charlie pulled her hands from the mound and leaned against the seat. "I remember reading *Little Dorrit* when I was in college. I remember the professor saying that Dickens had used Marshalsea—the debtors' prison—as the setting because that's where Dickens's father had served time."

"Right. Everyone in the family *but* Charles went into the prison with John. Charles was forced to sell off his beloved books and then work in a blacking factory. They say the abuse he took while there scarred him for the rest of his life. *But* he clearly found a peaceable path with his father, and he also never forgot the poor."

"Meaning, sometimes you have to take the trash life dumps on you and turn it into treasure for someone else?" Charlie crossed her arms. "And how do you suppose I do that?"

"For starters, you're helping us with the show. The money, as you know, is going to the homeless shelter—"

"Which, apparently, John is a part of."

"John..." Dusty seemed to ponder the name. "Do you realize that your father's name is John, and Dickens's father's name was John?" He smiled. "*And* your name is Charlie and his, Charles?"

Snarkiness rose inside her. "Well, God bless us, every one."

"Charlie..."

"Sorry."

He looked at his phone. "Man. I gotta get." But he drank her in all the same. "Are you going to be all right?"

"Yeah."

He slid from the bench seat and pulled a few bills from his wallet. "Hey..."

She looked to his face as he dropped the money on the table.

"Want to have dinner with me on Friday?"

Charlie nodded, too emotionally stretched to speak.

"Pick you up at seven?"

She nodded again. His fingertips lightly stroked her chin. "Call if you need me."

"Okay," she whispered.

Charlie waited a good minute after he left before reaching into her purse for her phone. As soon as she hit the Home button, a line of messages she'd somehow missed covered the screen. She checked the side of the phone; it had been bumped to silent. "Oh, my goodness." She read the first message. "Ashlynne...Ashlynne...Sis...Sis...Ashlynne..."

She called Ashlynne first. "I'm so sorry," she said as soon as the words "Where are you?" met her ear. "I know I said I'd be late, but then something came up. Important, of course. I wouldn't leave you stranded for no good reason and I—I'm so—I'm actually at The Spinning Bean. Are you still there?"

"No, but we can reschedule for tomorrow. I got them to hold a few pieces for us."

"Sounds good."

"And I called your grandmother. She's frantic, I'm afraid."

Charlie sighed. "I'm sure. I'll call her now."

She ended the call, then dialed Sis who answered immediately, as usual without a formal greeting. "I know you ran into your father," she said, her voice filled with authoritative disappointment. "He's nearly beside himself. Charlie, I raised you better than this."

"I know." Charlie dropped her forehead into the palm of her hand. "I'm sorry, Sis. I ran into Dusty, and we went to The Spinning Bean. I'm leaving now. I—"

"I'll let John know."

Wonderful. As long as she didn't have to speak to him.

"I'm on my way home." *Practically.* She grabbed her purse and slid out of the booth. "I'm leaving The Bean now." She stopped halfway to the door. "Wait. Is he—*there*?"

10

―∞∞―

"Spirit, conduct me where you will. I went forth last night on compulsion, and I learnt a lesson which is working now. To-night, if you have aught to teach me, let me profit by it."

—Ebenezer Scrooge

Sis sighed audibly. "Charlie, you are in no position right now to have this argument with me."

"Sis, please. I'm not ready for this."

"Well, young lady, you get ready. I'm not happy with you right now. Not one iota."

Charlie pushed through the door and onto the sidewalk where a bitter wind slapped her, nearly sending her backward. She shivered, wishing she'd worn more than a sweater. Then again, when she'd left home, the sun was bright and warm. Now it had dipped behind the mountains, shedding scant light and little heat. "Sis, I'm *sorry*. I'm coming home. But I'm not ready. *Please.* Ask him to leave."

She turned the corner and spied her car parked alone in front of the secondhand store. She glanced again at the sign, and the store's name hit her nearly as hard as the wind had. "I know you want me to just jump right into this, but I need a little time to process it. To think about it. To pray about it."

Her grandmother was so quiet she wondered if perhaps the line had gone dead. Or worse, that Sis had hung up on her.

"Sis?"

"He wanted to go out tonight and look for a tree." Her voice came through the phone whisper soft and low. "He wanted—he said—he told me the three of you used to go out every year. You'd come home and have hot cocoa and decorate the tree, and you'd laugh as he and your mother sang Christmas songs."

All that was true. Yes. *Before.* When everything in life appeared good and precious and easy to understand. When spring came in colors of pink and summer sprouted green and autumn turned gold and winter fell white. Now, everything had fallen into murky brown, clouded in gray.

Charlie slid into her car and started the engine. "Sis, I'm about to back the car up." The call went to the Bluetooth, and she threw her phone onto the passenger's seat. Charlie placed the gearshift into Reverse. "You don't like me to drive and talk on the phone, remember?"

"I'll see you in fifteen minutes then." Her grandmother's words were terse but certain.

Charlie pulled out of the parking place, then shifted to Drive, which automatically started her satellite radio. Mannheim Steamroller's version of "God Rest Ye Merry, Gentlemen" neared its final chords.

"Man," she said into the dusk around her. She loved that version of the song almost as much as she'd come to enjoy the one by Barenaked Ladies. "Missed it."

The light turned green, and she continued on as the DJ began his spiel about the song. "*Love* that version of the old classic," he said. "Now here's a little trivia for you about a song that's been known by several titles, including 'Tidings of Comfort and Joy,' 'Come All You Worthy Gentlemen,' and 'God Rest Ye, Merry Christians.' If you're a fan of Dickens's *A Christmas Carol*, which was written some hundred years after we *believe* this particular carol to have been written, you know that old Ebenezer Scrooge becomes characteristically upset when he hears a caroler singing the tune." The DJ chuckled as Charlie's eyes darted across the street, taking in as best she could the city's newest Christmas lights, and the old English lanterns that now outlined and lit the park. In its center, a life-sized crèche had been erected.

She'd not seen it before. Nor had she seen the sign that arched over it: "For God So Loved the World."

"Now a little bit about the Dickens classic..." the DJ continued.

Charlie shook her head. "Why can't I get away from this thing?" she asked out loud, even as she smiled around her misery.

"If you've read the story—"

"I have."

"—then you know that sometimes Ebenezer reads like a crotchety old geezer and other times he seems nice enough. You know, like when he's with the Ghost of Christmas Past and the Ghost of Christmas Present and the Ghost of Christmas Yet to Come. *Anyhoo*, there are theories that Dickens, who had a tumultuous relationship with his father—I guess you could call him a sort of con artist—"

"Sort of?"

"—created Scrooge based on the two personalities he knew of his father: the saint he loved and the demon he despised."

Charlie's heartbeat revved, forcing her to slow the car and ease onto the shoulder. Her breath came in gasps. Lights from an oncoming car lit her car from behind. A look in the rearview mirror revealed wild eyes—her own, hardly recognizable.

The car then drove around her, returning the interior to darkness as the DJ continued. "Speaking of Christmas *ghosts*, how about a little song by Johnny Mathis, eh? 'It's the Most Wonderful Time of the Year.'" He chuckled as the music started, and Charlie's heart slowed as the DJ stretched out the next sentence. "Scary ghost stories. Yep. I remember how *A Christmas Carol* used to scare me silly. But let's listen to the smooth voice of Mr. Mathis."

11

—⊗⊗⊗—

"Why, it's old Fezziwig! Bless his heart; it's Fezziwig alive again! [Mr. Fezziwig] has the power to render us happy or unhappy; to make our service light or burdensome; a pleasure or a toil.... The happiness he gives, is quite as great as if it cost a fortune."

—*Ebenezer Scrooge*

Charlie turned into the driveway to find Sis standing near the end of it.

She slammed on the brakes while rolling down the passenger's side window, her thumb seeking the radio's volume control on the steering wheel. "*Sis*. What are you doing out here? You'll catch your death."

Sis opened the car door and slid in while a tune from Straight No Chaser faded to silence. "I thought this way we could talk."

Charlie looked down the length of the driveway. The porch light revealed John's car parked in the front, next to his mother's. "He's still here."

"Charlie..." Sis turned to look at her. "I love you more than my bright red Keds, and you know how much I adore those shoes. I'm not about to force you to do anything you don't want to do."

Charlie placed her hand over her grandmother's. "It's okay, Sis. I love you that much, too, and I owe you so much."

Sis wrapped their hands with her own, much as Dusty had earlier. "You don't owe me anything, Charlie. But you owe *yourself* something."

"I do, too, owe you. A lot of grandmothers out there—believe me—don't even communicate with their granddaughters, much less take them in. I *know*, Sis, about the sacrifices you made, and I know about how you told John to leave me alone until I'd grown up." She paused as Sis's eyes grew wide. "I heard you once when I was younger," she explained. "You telling him to leave me be."

Sis chuckled. "Well, yes, I did. Then he went back to prison, but Charlie, I never stopped talking to him. I never stopped praying for him. He's my *son*."

"I know," she whispered.

"I'll always love him. Always believe in him. It's what love does."

"'Love is patient,'" Charlie quoted the memorized words from First Corinthians. "'Always trusts, always hopes.'"

"'Always perseveres,'" Sis finished. "'Love *never* fails.'"

"If that's true, Sis, then why did my parents—why *didn't* they...?"

"They loved you, Charlie. They still do. And they surely didn't mean to fail *you*. They only *meant* to fail themselves."

Charlie looked down the lane again, spying the outline of her father standing on the porch. "Maybe like John Dickens?"

Sis squeezed their hands, and Charlie turned back. "You've heard the story then?"

Charlie nodded.

"Let him *try*, Charlie," Sis said, looking at the figure they were both now aware of.

"I can do that."

"Can you?" Relief from Sis's voice filled the car.

Charlie forced herself to laugh. "Well...'love perseveres.'"

They took John's car to Brower's Christmas Tree Farm.

He didn't have satellite radio, but he'd brought along a CD—a homemade montage of Trans-Siberian Orchestra's holiday·music he'd created from his collection of the group's music.

"I love this music," Charlie blurted from the backseat, where she'd demanded to sit. "It's jazzy and vibrant."

Sis shook her head. "I'm getting a headache," she said, and John immediately turned down the volume on "Wish Liszt."

"Sorry, Mom. I forgot how much you like the more classic carols."

"Don't worry about me," Sis said, feigning weariness. "*Charlie* likes contemporary."

"Do you?" John glanced into the rearview mirror, his eyes focused on Charlie, who sat behind him. "Your mother always loved the standards."

Charlie shrugged, not wanting to get too comfortable talking about *the good ole days*. "I like the standards, too. I listen to satellite radio in my car. The Holly Station? They play a variety..."

"But she's not crazy about *A Christmas Carol*," Sis added.

"What is this?" Charlie coughed a laugh. "Abuse Charlie night? Besides, that's not what I said. *What I said was* that I think it's been done to death. I have nothing against it *personally*."

The CD changed to another track; the opening measures of "A Mad Russian's Christmas" started. "Oh, I love this one," Charlie said.

"Not sure your grandmother will like it if I turn it too loud," her father said, and she noted the merriment in his eyes.

"Don't mind me," Sis said, her head turning to gaze out the window at they drove past silhouettes of trees and over-grown brush. "I'm just an old woman who won't have her hearing much longer anyway."

"And I'm a pirate with a peg leg," John teased back.

Charlie bit her lip to keep from laughing. How dare he make her smile.

Two songs later, they pulled up beside a nearly rusted-out army-green Chevy, the name "Brower's Christmas Tree Farm" painted without blemish on the side doors. "You'd think ole Sal would have bought a new truck by now instead of just updating the sign on the paint," her father said as he turned the key in the ignition.

"I think he drove this truck back when I was in high school," Charlie added.

"You two stop," Sis said as she opened her door. "The Browers don't have a lot, what with all the kids they have to feed. Sometimes you have to choose between fancy wheels and peanut butter."

Charlie shook her head and reached for the door handle. Before she could grasp it, her father opened her door from the outside. He shivered dramatically as she exited. "I hope you're going to be warm enough. It's turning colder by the minute."

Charlie tightened her scarf, then shoved her leather-gloved hands into her coat pockets to bring it more tightly around her. "I'm fine," she muttered, hoping he didn't try something prematurely, like putting an arm around her shoulder or something.

Instead, he looked out over the scene—the strings of large white light bulbs bordering a forest of six- to eight-foot firs, pines, and spruces. The overpowering scent of the greenery blended with the chatter of other customers and the laughter of children who ran between the trunks and branches.

Charlie smiled as she joined her grandmother, who *did* loop her arm through Charlie's. They drew close as a teenage girl with oversized glasses and long white-blonde hair pulled back in a tight ponytail greeted them at the entrance. She held a wood-handled handsaw toward John, who'd caught up to walk next to Sis. "Here you go," she said. Next to her, a CD player played Tchaikovsky's *Nutcracker Suite.*

"The prices are on the little signs hanging off the branches." She smiled, displaying large teeth. "Hi, there, Mrs. Dixon," she said to Sis.

"Gwen."

She turned to Charlie. "Hi, Miss Dixon."

"Hi." Charlie recognized the girl as a Brower—they all looked pretty much alike—but felt there was something even more familiar about her.

"Gwen," Sis continued, "I'm so happy you've decided to take the role of Fred's wife in the play."

Ah…

"I envy the range of your singing voice," Sis continued.

The girl pinked, although it might also have been from a sudden slap of cold wind that sliced around the rows of trees. "Thank you, Mrs. Dixon. I admit to being a little nervous about singing in front of so many strangers."

Sis patted the girl's hand, covered in a knitted mitten that appeared to have seen better days. Charlie's fingers twitched within the fine leather of her gloves, fully aware of her blessings in spite of the day's events. "You have no reason to be." She looked into the crowd of trees and townspeople. "Oh, look. There's Doris Tomlin."

Gwen looked into the crowd, as did Charlie. "She's here with her grandkids," Gwen supplied. "Including snooty Tina," she finished, muttering.

Charlie looked back to Gwen. She understood. Teaching at Miss Fisher's had made her keenly aware of cliques and clubs and bullying girls.

Realizing other people now stood behind them, Charlie looked at her father. "You've got the saw?"

He held it up. "Ready and able."

She smiled at Gwen. "We'll be back shortly, Gwen."

The three walked into the forest of trees. "That's a nice one," Sis said, pointing to practically the first tree on the lot.

"Too skinny, Mom," John commented. They continued on, saying nothing, when Sis spotted another one and smiled.

"How about that one?" she asked.

"Too fat," John said. "It'll swallow the room."

"I feel like I'm in a fairy tale," Charlie mumbled. "Too hot, too cold, too hard, too soft...*just right*," she added, using her best Goldilocks voice.

"Tell you what, then," John challenged with a grin. "*You* pick the perfect tree." He waved the saw in the air. "And I'll do the cutting."

A memory washed over Charlie. Her mother. Her father. Herself—only a little girl. Her head covered by a wooly cap, her hands by fingerless mittens.

She ran between the trees, giggling as her father called, "Wait up, Charlie!"

"I'm finding the perfect tree," she hollered back, looking behind to see her parents walking hand in hand.

Then, without warning, she plunged shoulder first and full force into a monster of green needles and thick brown trunk.

"Charlie," her mother called out, hurrying to kneel beside her. "Are you all right, sweetheart?"

Charlie looked up, past her mother's pretty face, to catch the fullness of the moon shining through the branches, illuminating each and every one as though by magic. Squashing her embarrassment at such a tumble, she mumbled, "I'm okay, but I think the perfect tree has found me."

John looked at her expectantly, as if he remembered too...and how it had taken both him and a family friend who happened by to cut the tree and then tote it to the front for purchase. When they'd made it home, the tree had "swallowed the room," rather than the other way around. Gayle had laughed over the lack of ornaments, calling it "a Charlie Brown Christmas in the Dixon household." But they'd strung popcorn and cranberries and hung candy canes and tinsel. And when they were finished, the tree had been worthy of a *Southern Living* cover.

"Don't tell me you're going to try to run into another tree today," John whispered.

Charlie laughed nervously as Sis stared at the two of them, both caught in the memory and held there by something precious and—almost—*tender.*

"What are you two talking about?" she asked.

"The monster tree," Charlie said. She turned, her eyes gazing over the rows on both sides until she spotted one large enough to duplicate, but not so large they wouldn't fit it through the door. "That one," she said, pointing.

John handed the saw to his mother, then dared Charlie, "Race you."

Without hesitation, father and daughter took off in a run with Sis calling, "Slow down before you hurt someone."

Charlie reached the tree first, and she snatched the price tag from one of the limbs. "Oh," she said, breathless. "Wow. That's more than I thought."

John took the card from her hand. "I got it," he said.

"Da—Dad." Charlie swallowed hard behind the name. "No."

Her father blinked, then scanned the height of the Fraser Fir. "Some beauty, though."

Sis arrived then. "If the tree I pointed to was too big, then this one..."

"I was wrong, Mom."

"How much?" she asked.

"You don't want to know," Charlie mumbled.

"I. Have. Got. It." John glared at them both. "No arguments. Charlie, hold the tree right here," he said, pointing between the center branches. "Mom? The saw?"

Cutting the tree became a comedy of errors, laced with laughter. Occasionally, Charlie caught a glimpse of her grandmother's face, noting the reflection of joy. Maybe spending the evening with her father wasn't so bad, she reckoned, especially if it meant Sis's happiness.

As they left, Charlie lingered behind the figure of her father dragging the tree toward his car and the voice of her grandmother declaring, "It's going to scratch the top of your car to bits," as John laughed.

"Don't worry, Mom. I brought an old blanket."

She stopped at the entrance where Gwen stood over the CD player, struggling to exchange one holiday disk for another with her worn-mittened hands.

Charlie pulled the expensive gloves she'd splurged on the year before from her fingers. "They're just too tight," she exclaimed.

Gwen looked up. "Oh, hi." Then looking at the gloves, she said, "Gosh, those are nice."

Charlie clutched them in one fist. "But too tight. I thought my hands were going to fall off while we were cutting the tree." She looked at Gwen's hands. "Say . . . yours look smaller than mine. Try them on and see if they fit."

Gwen's fingers shook as she reached for the gloves, and she breathed out, "Are you sure?"

"Try them," Charlie said with a shrug. "If they fit, they're yours."

She smiled as the girl's hands slid in easily. Perfectly.

"Oh my goodness. They feel like a million bucks." Gwen wiggled her fingers.

"Not quite," Charlie said. "But they're cashmere lined." She caught the girl's eyes with her own. "Be careful with them, okay? They're only for you."

Gwen nodded. "I promise." She grinned wider. "Merry Christmas, Miss Dixon."

"You, too, Gwen. See you soon."

12

———⚬⚬⚬———

During the whole of this time, Scrooge had acted
like a man out of his wits. His heart and soul were
in the scene, and with his former self. He corrobo-
rated everything, remembered everything, enjoyed
everything, and underwent the strangest agitation.
It was not until now, when the bright faces of his
former self and Dick were turned from them, that
he remembered the Ghost, and became conscious
that it was looking full upon him, while the light
upon its head burnt very clear.

Did you meet with Ashlynne yesterday?" Dusty asked as he walked Charlie from the side porch to his car.

She nodded. "Finally. We picked up quite a few things. For the rest, we'll have to get with—who did Ashlynne say?—somebody who sews the costumes for them each year."

"Miss Anise...um, Anise Carver." Dusty opened the passenger door for her, standing so close she could smell the mints on his breath mixing headily with his aftershave and the leather of his jacket. "This is my first year, too, so I haven't met her yet."

"Mm-hmm," she answered, unable to fully speak. She'd waited for this moment since fifth grade. She didn't want to waste a moment of the memory it would hold for her later by talking about someone neither of them knew.

She slid into the car and adjusted her seat belt and purse while Dusty ran around to the other side and got in, rubbing his hands together. Charlie pulled her hair, now unbraided and curled, from beneath the seat belt.

"Can you believe how cold it's gotten?" he asked as he shut the door behind him. "I don't ever remember it being this cold so early in December."

Charlie threw a smile his way. "Maybe we'll have a white Christmas."

"You know what would be completely cool?" He turned the key and started the car. "If it snowed the night of the play. It'd be like—well, it would be like a Dickens Christmas."

"Would we still be able to have the play?"

Dusty's eyes grew wide. "We'd better."

"Which reminds me," Charlie said as they neared the highway. "Why in the world did you choose to have the performance on the *nineteenth* of all nights? Why not a Friday night? Or a Saturday matinee?"

Dusty steered the car away from town and increased the speed. "The book was released on December 19, 1843. Can you think of a better date?"

Charlie did the math. "Nearly a hundred and seventy-five years ago."

Dusty nodded. "Give or take a year."

"Pretty amazing when you think about it." She pressed her lips together, tasting the strawberry gloss she'd glided over her lips moments before Dusty arrived at the house. "That a book has been a best seller *all this time.*"

"And to think ole Charles had to fund the thing with what little bit of money he had in his accounts." He turned his head to look at her briefly, then sent his attention back to the curves in the dark road ahead of them. "You look pretty tonight, by the way."

Heat rose through her, beginning at her toes and ending with warmth in her cheeks. "Thank you," she said, almost too embarrassed to be polite.

"I don't think I've ever seen you with your hair down." Dusty glanced her way again. Back to the road. "Or wearing makeup."

Charlie studied the curve in the road. "Where are you taking me?"

"Change of subject, huh?"

"If you don't mind," she said, crossing her arms and laughing. "Honestly, I never knew my hair and makeup were of such notable interest."

"I'm a man," he shot back. "I notice these things."

She inhaled sharply. Swiping gloss over her lips and mascara over her lashes had been the most she'd done in preparation that evening, but it was decidedly more than she did most days. If Sis had said it once, she'd said it a thousand times: "You're a natural beauty, Charlie. What do you need with all that goop?"

Like grandmother, like granddaughter.

Even in high school, as her friends experimented with crazy nail polish, eye shadows, and blushes, the most Charlie had done was apply clear gloss to her nails. But tonight. Tonight felt different. Tonight she and Dusty were going out to dinner. *Finally.*

The car moved between the expanse of foliage and fields as the shadows of the mountains rose before them. "Lake Lure?" Charlie finally asked. "I mean, if you aren't going to answer me, I may as well dig deeper with my sharp methods of investigation."

Dusty laughed. "Oh, yeah? What methods are those? Bright light in my eyes? No water until I break?"

"No," Charlie answered with a giggle. "I simply ask questions like any normal female."

Dusty opened his mouth to speak, then closed it briefly before saying, "You're far from *normal*, Charlie Dixon."

"Is that a compliment?"

"It is."

"Then, thank you."

"You're welcome. And yes. Lake Lure."

"La Strada?"

"More of your devious questions?"

She grinned. "Yes."

"Well, yeah. But how'd you know? Don't tell me female intuition."

"No. We save that for the really important things. It was a guess, really."

"Good guess."

Together they said, "I love their pizza."

After their laughter subsided, the conversation grew quiet again. Then Dusty cleared his throat and spoke into the silence. "Have I mentioned you look pretty tonight?"

He held her hand, fingers intertwined as he walked her to the cottage's side door.

They'd said so little as they neared the house, Charlie wondered if the same butterflies that had taken over her stomach had also fluttered in his. Her tongue darted over the freshly applied strawberry gloss, then quickly returned to her mouth. She didn't want to *assume* a kiss dangled on the horizon, but it sure would be nice.

A kiss. From Dusty Kennedy.

Merry Christmas to me.

"Hey," he said, pulling her from her holiday wish. They stopped shy of the steps, turning to each other. "What are you doing tomorrow night?"

Instant joy shot through her, then fizzled. "Oh. Um— we're—Sis, my father, and me—we're decorating the tree." Her eyes widened. "Why don't you and Jeremy come over and be a part of it?"

Say yes, say yes.

Disappointment became a shadow on his face. "No, no. We wouldn't want to intrude."

She couldn't let him go that easily. "If I thought you were intruding, I wouldn't ask you." Charlie put on her best smile. "Besides, Sis really puts on the dog on the night we decorate. She always has." She blinked. "I think, mostly in the early years—you know, after my parents went to prison—it was to make sure I had some sense of home and happiness."

"Still, I—"

"Oh, say yes. Jeremy shouldn't greet the new year without having seen Sis wearing her blinking reindeer antlers."

Dusty appeared amused at the thought, sending new hope through Charlie.

She leaned in close. "Say yes," she pleaded. "It'll be fun. And what with this being my first year decorating a tree with my—with Jo—with—Dad since I was only a little older than Jeremy, maybe you can help kiss—I mean *kill* some of my anxiety."

"I like the kissing part better than the killing part."

Heat rose through her. "I wasn't—"

"Shh," he said, leaning in to press his lips gently against hers.

Charlie's eyes fluttered and closed as her arms went over his shoulders as his slid around her waist, drawing her closer without stepping over any boundaries of propriety. When he ended the kiss, she stepped back, opened her eyes slowly, and whispered, "Do you know how long I've waited for that?"

He pressed his forehead against hers, laughed lightly, and said, "No, Strawberry Shortcake. How long?"

She swallowed, feeling herself blush at his endearment. "How old are we now?"

Dusty laughed harder. "Don't you know?"

"Not at this moment, no."

He kissed her again briefly. "Twenty-seven."

"Oh. Yeah." Their eyes met. Locked. She licked her lips, tasting faint berries blended with the complimentary mint they'd been given after their meal. The one he'd popped into his mouth as they'd neared home. "Well, I met you when I was ten. So, seventeen years."

"That's a long time to wait for a kiss," he whispered before abruptly drawing back. "Wait. You wanted me to kiss you when we were *ten*?"

She nodded. "I would have been happy with a note—I like you, do you like me?—passed between Mrs. Jenkins's class and Mr. Solomon's."

Dusty threw back his head and laughed. "Good ole Mr. Solomon. Never in the history of Testament Elementary School was there ever a more Scrooge-like teacher." Then, looking at her again, his eyes tender, he asked. "So? Do you?"

"Do I what?"

"Like me?"

Charlie diverted her attention to the screen door where Sis had recently hung a Christmas wreath, now gathering frost. "I do." Her eyes made her way back to his. "Do you?"

"I do."

Silence settled between them.

"So then? Tomorrow night?" she asked, hopeful.

"What time?"

"Seven."

"You'll also be at rehearsal tomorrow afternoon, right?"

"Of course. One o'clock. We're practicing in the music room."

"We'll be in the auditorium." Dusty took a step back, running his hands down Charlie's arms, sending shivers in their wake. When his hands linked with hers, he said, "Let's plan the last half hour to bring the two groups together to go over the format a little more."

Charlie nodded, torn between anticipation and disappointment. Had it been necessary for their conversation to leave teasing and flirtation? Must they talk business already? Had he regretted the moments they'd shared? "Sounds good," she choked out. Why had she told him about her feelings from so long ago?

Dusty raised a brow. "Are you sure?"

"Mm-hmm." She pulled her hands from his. "I should—I should go in before Sis does something horrible. You know, like flicker the porch light."

This time his brow knitted together. "Oh. Okay." He shoved his hands into his jacket pockets. "Getting cold anyway."

Charlie went up two of the steps and clasped the brass door handle. "Thank you for dinner."

"Sure." He walked toward the car. "See you tomorrow then?"

She nodded, opened the door, and stepped inside.

13

Perhaps it was the pleasure the good Spirit had in showing off this power of his, or else it was his own kind, generous, hearty nature, and his sympathy with all poor men, that led him straight to Scrooge's clerk's; for there he went, and took Scrooge with him, holding to his robe; and on the threshold of the door the Spirit smiled, and stopped to bless Bob Cratchit's dwelling with the sprinkling of his torch. Think of that! Bob had but fifteen "Bob" a-week himself; he pocketed on Saturdays but fifteen copies of his Christian name; and yet the Ghost of Christmas Present blessed his four-roomed house!

What do you mean?"

Ashlynne stood on one side of the table near the back of the music room fifteen minutes before the carolers were to arrive. A bin—open and in the center—held fabric and the recently purchased Victorianesque wraps, gloves, and hats. With her hair pulled back in a high ponytail and her makeup expertly worn, she looked so much like a Barbie doll, Charlie had to smile in spite of the seriousness in her voice.

"Ashlynne, in one second flat, he shifted from flirting with me and kissing me to talking about the play." Charlie blew into her cupped hand. "*Italian* food. Maybe it was my breath. I can still smell the pizza."

Ashlynne shook her head as she placed the thread they'd bought earlier into the bin. She'd take it to the seamstress that afternoon. "Charlie, really." She chuckled. "One thing I've learned about men in the short while I've been married is that they put their thoughts in boxes."

"What?"

Ashlynne looked around the room, then walked to a shelf where several sheet music containers had been placed. She stacked them and brought them over to the table, then set one beside the other.

"See these?"

Charlie nodded.

"*This*," she said, waving her hands over the table, "represents a man's brain. Inside his brain are little boxes." She pointed to one box. "See this one? We'll call this box *Finances*. Inside this box, a man thinks about *money*. See this one?" She pointed to another one.

Charlie smiled. "Let me guess. Women?"

"And all that entails," Ashlynne said, her hand resting on the swell of her stomach. "Good. Now you're getting it." She took a deep breath. "So, a man can only think inside one box at a time. Us? We can think about ten different things at once. Our brains are like—how did Will once put it?— worms in a wet dirt bed."

Charlie burst out laughing. "So what you're saying," she added when she'd sobered, "is that last night Dusty was in *this* box." She pointed to the second box. "And then he shifted—for some odd reason—to *this* box." She pointed to the bin holding the costumes.

"You have now graduated from Man 101."

"Then I shouldn't have taken it personally. Or worried that I'd scared him off with my declaration of a lifetime crush."

"I sincerely don't think so." Ashlynne returned the boxes to the shelf. "Are you ready for me to take the fabric and patterns and stuff to Miss Anise?"

Charlie glanced at her watch. "Yeah. The singers will be here in about fifteen minutes."

Ashlynne secured the green top to the bin and slid it toward her.

"Let me do that," Charlie said. "You shouldn't be lifting anything so heavy."

Ashlynne raised the bin. "Give me some credit here. It weighs approximately three pounds."

"Seriously. Let me," Charlie insisted, taking the clear bin from her. "I'll walk you to your car."

"All right then." She looked toward the front of the classroom. "I'll get the door."

"The very least you can do," Charlie teased.

She was halfway back from Ashlynne's car when she rounded one of the outside corridors and ran—literally—straight into Dusty. For a moment, they were a fumble of hands and heads. Then, after righting themselves, Dusty managed to say, "I see you made it."

"I did." Charlie felt a tender blush rising through her. "I met Ashlynne up here a little while ago to get things together for the seamstress. I'm a little worried she won't have time to sew the costumes my singers are wearing for the performance." She paused. "Why are you staring at me like that?"

"Like what?"

"Like what box are you in right now?"

"What?"

Charlie waved her hands between them. "Nothing. A little joke. A bad one."

Dusty reached over and tugged at the thick braid falling over her shoulder. "You're back to the braid."

She pointed to her face. "And no makeup."

He rested his hands on his hips. "And you still look pretty."

Charlie grinned. "I do?"

"Mm-hmm. Amazing."

Charlie struggled for something to say, settling on, "Well, I'd best get to the classroom. I'll see you at what? Three thirty?"

Dusty pulled his cell phone from his hip pocket to check it. "Yeah. Sounds good. Just bring the singers over to the auditorium then."

They cautiously moved around each other. When they'd separated by a few feet, Dusty said, "Oh and—"

Charlie turned. "Yes?"

"Jeremy is really looking forward to tonight."

She smiled. "So is Sis. She said it's been a long time since we've had a child in the house. And, you know, there's something magical about all that."

Dusty smiled back. "That there is. Yes, ma'am."

Charlie's father arrived at five o'clock—only fifteen minutes after Sis and Charlie returned from rehearsals—toting a platter full of sliced baked ham. He presented it like a peace offering as soon as he entered. "Not sure what you had planned, Mom, but I figured I'd add to it with this."

Sis lifted the clear plastic wrap and inhaled. "Gracious, but doesn't that smell good."

Charlie stood across the room, her stomach churning at the aroma. "How about I open a jar of applesauce and heat it up?"

"With some little English peas?" John asked his mother.

Sis took the platter. "This will be the easiest meal ever," she said, placing it on the breakfast nook table. "And here I wondered what in the world I was going to fix."

Charlie went to the pantry and pulled out the jar of applesauce. "We've been at rehearsals all day. Sis worked with the actors, and I worked with the singers."

Her father began opening overhead cabinets. "Where's your cinnamon?"

"Over there," Sis answered, pointing.

"So?" he asked, retrieving the spice. "How's it going?"

Charlie busied herself warming the applesauce and opening a can of sweet peas while Sis and John sat at the table with mugs of coffee between them, and Sis gave a detailed report on the show.

"Oh," Charlie said from the stove, "and Dusty and Jeremy are coming over tonight to help with the tree."

Sis winked at her son. "I think we *may* have a romance blooming."

John straightened. "Do we now?"

Charlie returned to stirring the applesauce and adding pats of butter to the peas. The last thing she needed—wanted, really—from her father was a sudden "daddy-kins" attitude. They'd only just begun speaking again. She'd let down her guard, but she didn't want him thinking he could interrogate Dusty the minute he walked in the door. "Can we *not* go there?" she asked, keeping her focus on the food preparation.

"Of course not," Sis said.

John slapped his hands together. "Okay, then. Change of subject. I had another meeting today with the manager of A Second Chance. Since there's no homeless shelter here in Testament, they're organizing with the Board of Education to bring a busload of folks—homeless or simply poor—from here to Morganton for Christmas dinner. We'll use the proceeds from the play to cover the costs. We're figuring about a hundred to a hundred and fifty men, women, and children for the meal."

Charlie turned. "That many?"

John wrapped his hand around the coffee mug and brought it to his lips. "Could be more. We'll have an exact number as we get closer to the twenty-fifth."

"I had no idea," Charlie breathed out, then turned to reduce both burners to low. She joined her father and grandmother at the table, choosing the chair next to Sis. "Seriously. No idea."

"About what?" her father asked her. "The number of indigent in our two towns?"

"Yes. I mean—"

John looked at his mother. "I'm only grateful that Mom came up with the idea of joining forces and using the money from the play. I had no idea where or how I was going to come up with the funds to feed even the folks from our shelter on Christmas." He winked across the table. "We figure at five dollars for an individual ticket and ten dollars per family, we should make around fifteen hundred to two grand. Maybe more."

"It will go a long way," Sis added, "toward feeding those kind souls, and you should still have a little left over."

"I guess living in the loveliness of Miss Fisher's, I stopped thinking about how the other half lives."

John blew on his coffee before taking a swallow, then returned the mug to the table. "Hey, I have an idea," he said, looking at Charlie.

"What's that?"

"What are you doing Monday?"

14

—∞∞∞—

There was nothing of high mark in this. They were
not a handsome family; they were not well dressed;
their shoes were far from being water-proof; their
clothes were scanty; and Peter might have known,
and very likely did, the inside of a pawnbroker's.
But, they were happy, grateful, pleased with one
another, and contented with the time; and when
they faded, and looked happier yet in the bright
sprinklings of the Spirit's torch at parting, Scrooge
had his eye upon them, and especially on Tiny Tim,
until the last.

Charlie topped the frothy hot cocoa in the five Christmas mugs lined up on the kitchen counter with miniature marshmallows. As she completed the garnishment, Dusty quietly took each one and placed it on a tray decorated with Frosty the Snowman's face.

"I've heard rumors about this hot cocoa," he said, reaching for the third cup.

Charlie looked at him. "Oh?"

"Yeah. Remember Janie Gray?"

"From high school? Of course. She and I were pretty good friends." Charlie added the final handful of marshmallows. "Wonder whatever happened to her."

"She moved to Canada to work for some hotshot company. Got married. Has two kids. Boy and girl."

Charlie shot him a look. "What? You don't have her exact street address?"

"Facebook," he answered. "We touch base every so often."

"Didn't you date her for a while?" Charlie asked casually as though she didn't know the answer. She picked up the last mug and handed it to Dusty.

Mischief sparkled in his eyes as he added it to the tray. "Don't give me that. You know good and well..."

Charlie grinned. "Okay. Okay. Janie Gray."

Dusty looped his fingers in the handle of one of the mugs and brought it to his lips. He blew slowly, sending the marshmallows to the other side. "She told me," he said, then took a sip. Swallowed. "Oh, my gracious goodness." He blew again. "She was right. This *is* amazing."

Charlie picked up the tray. "Old family recipe. I'd give it to you, but then I'd be forced to kill you."

"Ha ha."

Charlie carried the tray into the living room where Sis and her father, aided by Jeremy, carefully removed ornaments from a holiday storage bin.

"And this one," Sis explained to Jeremy as she produced a brass impression of a little drummer boy, "belonged to Mister John when he was a little boy." She pointed to the base of the ornament. "See his name there?"

"J-O-H-N," Jeremy said.

Charlie placed the tray of cocoa on the coffee table. Dusty plucked up the one with the least amount of liquid and took it to his son. "Here, buddy. Try this."

Jeremy wrapped both hands around it and gingerly sipped from the mug. "Mm," he said, licking his lips.

"Careful now. It's hot. Blow like Daddy showed you."

Charlie sat on the sofa and smiled, remembering similar moments with her own father. "Dad?" she said, still uncomfortable with the title. "Want yours now?" She reached for her own and crossed her legs.

John stretched. "Think I will."

Sis added the ornament to the tree. "I say it's time for a break anyway."

Charlie turned from her place on the sofa to look at the tree. "How am I supposed to enjoy the tree when it's *behind* me?" she asked.

"The point is," John began, "for *Santa* to see the tree's lights from the neighbor's roof, not for *you* to see the tree." He ruffled Jeremy's hair. "Right, sport?"

Jeremy tilted his beaming face toward John, a circle of cocoa around his lips. "Right."

Sis sat in her rocker. "I can see it just fine."

"Mmm," Charlie teased. Then looking again at the tree, she added, "I've got the cranberries and popcorn for stringing. I just have to pop the corn." She stood.

"Let me help," Dusty said as she started out. "I'm a master popcorn popper."

Charlie stared at him. "It's microwave."

He shrugged. "I'm a master microwave popcorn popper."

"Go on, you two," Sis said. "We've got this in here."

Charlie pulled a box of popcorn and three bags of cranberries from the pantry, then handed the box to Dusty. "For you, Chef Dustin," she teased.

He looked at the bags. "I've never known anyone to actually string cranberries."

"It's a tradition that started when I was a little girl," she said. Then as she retrieved a large needle and the string, she told him about the monster tree.

Dusty placed the popcorn in the microwave and, after closing it, pressed the setting for Popcorn. He leaned against the counter, crossed his ankles, and crooked his finger.

"What?" Charlie said.

"Come here," he mouthed.

She came closer, and he wrapped her in his arms before planting a light kiss on the tip of her nose. "I like knowing these stories about you," he said.

"What about you? What stories of Christmas do you have? What traditions?"

He stood silently in thought, then said, "We always opened one gift on Christmas Eve." He chuckled. "When my brothers and I were little, we spent *days* cross-legged in front of the tree, trying to figure out *the best* gift to open first."

"That's a nice tradition. Is there a reason behind it?"

"Not really, no," he said over the rhythm of popping corn. "I'm sure my mother would like to say it has something to do with something or another, but the truth is I think she and my dad just liked that gathering together on Christmas Eve. We went to church, of course, for the candlelight service. Then home to dinner and pecan pie, after which my father would read the nativity story to us from the Book of Luke."

"I think," Charlie said as the microwave dinged, "that Christmas should be rich in remembrance of the birth of Jesus, blended with some of our traditional and modern traditions."

Dusty reached for the microwave's handle. "Traditional *and* modern, huh? Is this *really* the girl who rolled her eyes at the thought of *A Christmas Carol*?"

Charlie threw her hands up dramatically. "I *never* said I didn't like traditional. I only said—oh, never mind." She searched his face. "You're egging me on, aren't you?"

Dusty waved the bag of popcorn at her. "How many of these do you think we're going to need?"

"Let's start with three bags and see where we land." She paused, watching him place another bag in the microwave. "Hey," she added.

He looked at her. Closed the door.

"My father has asked me to go with him on Monday to see what it is he does."

Dusty pressed the Popcorn setting once again. "Oh?"

"I didn't say yes or no, but I think I'm going. I'd like to see what he does exactly." She shrugged one shoulder. "Maybe—I don't know—maybe I'll lose this uneasy feeling I haven't yet quite lost."

"Wise choice."

"I don't know, Dusty. I *want* to believe he's changed. I do. It's just—I learned a long time ago not to trust him. He didn't go to jail *once*. He went *back*—more than once. Don't you think some time should at least go by before we all relax and call him changed?"

Dusty crossed his arms in thought. "One time, when Jesus was talking to the disciples, he told them he was sending them out 'like sheep among wolves.'"

"'Therefore,'" Charlie finished, "'be as shrewd as snakes and as innocent as doves.'"

"Right. And that means there *are* wolves. I guess it's up to us, in our wisdom, to know the wolves from the puppies. *And* in the process, we're to remain teachable. Innocent."

"'If it is possible, as far as it depends on you, live—'"

Dusty chimed in for the last few words and said them with her: "at peace with everyone." Dusty added, "Romans 12:18." Then he said, "All you can do, Charlie, is give the man a chance. Meanwhile, keep your eyes and ears open. Jesus doesn't expect you to set yourself up for abuse. But, well, I keep thinking about the apostle Paul."

The microwave announced its completion once again, followed by three random pops from the bag. Dusty replaced the second bag with the third as he said, "You know. When he went from Saul to Paul, the disciples who were in Jerusalem didn't believe it at first. They thought he was—I don't know—a spy or something. They worried that the whole thing was a setup."

"Mm-hmm. I get that."

"What's the worst thing that could happen if you go, Charlie?"

"I'm not sure. I'd have to think about that." She paused. "I guess I could find out that he's a liar...and Sis would be devastated, Dusty. I couldn't bear that."

"But at least you'd know sooner rather than later, right?"

"I suppose."

"Now," he said as the last bag of popcorn popped in earnest. "What's the *best* thing that could happen?"

Charlie blinked. "The opposite, I suppose. I could find out he's telling the truth."

The microwave went into the final seconds of the cycle and dinged. "Either way, there's only one way to find out."

15

---⚬⚬⚬---

It is a fair, even-handed, noble adjustment of things, that while there is infection in disease and sorrow, there is nothing in the world so irresistibly contagious as laughter and good-humour. When Scrooge's nephew laughed in this way: holding his sides, rolling his head, and twisting his face into the most extravagant contortions: Scrooge's niece, by marriage, laughed as heartily as he. And their assembled friends being not a bit behindhand, roared out lustily.

Charlie rose long before sunup to have coffee and breakfast in the dark with Sis, then drove the forty-five minutes between Testament and Morganton, using her iPhone's GPS to locate the homeless shelter.

Her father had instructed her to drive around to the back of the building, through the alley. "You'll see my car. Park near it. Then rap on the back door and I'll hear you."

Sure enough, his instructions were spot-on. What he hadn't told her—explained to her, really—was the darkness of the location. Not so much by degree of light but by degree of humanity. Trash spilled from the Dumpsters, emitting a putrid odor. Rusted shopping carts stood here and there like discarded shoes. Paint chipped off buildings, which rose up around them to give the alley an even more claustrophobic feel.

Charlie tightened her scarf and tugged at the inexpensive knit mittens she'd purchased on Saturday in a cutesy gift shop in Testament. Looking down at her coat, she frowned. If she'd known earlier what she knew now, she'd have worn a less fashionable jacket.

She threw the shoulder strap of her purse over her arm, clutching it as she stared at the three doors facing her. She had no idea which one would lead to her father.

Charlie chose "Door Number Two."

After three knocks, it opened, revealing the face of a middle-aged woman, large eyes beaming. Her auburn hair had been pulled back into a ponytail and wrapped in a hairnet. She wore a stained bib apron that, Charlie guessed, might have been white at one time. Now it appeared trapped between gray and beige.

"You must be Charlie," she said, pushing the door open to allow Charlie to come in.

"I—I am." Charlie stepped into a room of shelves stacked with large cans of vegetables—green beans, whole kernel corn, potatoes—and bags of flour and sugar. She turned slowly.

"I'm Marie." The woman extended a slender hand.

Charlie took it in her gloved one and shook. "Nice to meet you." She turned, hoping to see her father.

"Your dad's run out for a minute. Told me to expect you." She nodded toward an open door on the far side of the room. "Come this way."

Charlie followed.

"Excuse the décor, or lack thereof," Marie said with a laugh. "Down there is your dad's office." Marie pointed to a tiny room at the end of a narrow hallway. "Let's put your coat and purse in there."

Charlie shrugged out of her coat as they walked into the office. "Will my—uh—will my purse be—"

Marie turned and smiled, her hand extended. "We'll lock it up tight in John's desk."

Charlie's eyes lingered over the paper-strewn, scarred desk. A framed photo of her as a child stood on one corner, the only decorative item in the entire room. "Oh," she said, not sure whether the response went to Marie's statement or to the shock of seeing her old fourth-grade school picture.

"Don't be embarrassed. I was a little uneasy my first day here, too."

First day? Charlie forced a smile in answer, hoping her father didn't expect this to be the first of many trips to Morganton.

"This way," Marie continued, "is the kitchen."

"Smells good," Charlie said as they entered the industrial room where several cooks stood over hot griddles, flipping bacon and pancakes and scrambling eggs. Across the room, three young women worked over sinks while another two lifted large trays of food and exited through a swinging door. Like Marie, they all wore the gray-beige aprons, and they all had their hair covered. "Wow!"

"We feed about fifty every morning," Marie said. "Except Saturdays and Sundays. Then the numbers go up. Of course, the ones you see now will be back at dinner with their children, who are able to eat breakfast at the school. We typically serve hot soup and homemade bread. During the day we provide a link to social services, that kind of thing. In the afternoons, we have a classroom where the children can do their homework."

"Really?"

"Hey, there," her father's voice interrupted. She turned to see him pulling a black bib apron over his head before securing it behind his back.

"Hey...Dad."

"Marie, would you get my daughter an apron and hairnet please?"

Charlie's hand went up to her head. "I—uh—"

"State regulations."

"Of course."

"Come with me," he said, turning her toward the swinging door. "We're down one server today. You don't mind, do you?"

"No, I—"

"I'll show you around after the breakfast rush. Explain things to you a little better."

Charlie shuffled out of the kitchen and into a large dining room where, on their side of the room, steam rose from a cafeteria-style row of food beneath a sneeze guard. The young women she'd seen earlier stood nearby, serving a row of men and women clad in layers of clothing. Charlie couldn't help noticing how their hands—wrapped in fingerless gloves—trembled as they gripped the sides of their plates, as if someone might come along at any moment to snatch them away.

"Ladies," John said, "this is my daughter, Charlie. Charlie—Dinah and Andrea. Girls, Charlie is going to fill in this morning."

Marie came up behind her. "Here you go. One bib just like your dad's and one hairnet." She threw the black bib over Charlie's head and tied the strings in the back while Charlie worked to get her braid into the net. "Easy enough," Marie said as John handed Charlie an industrial-sized serving spoon.

"You're on grits duty." He walked around the serving counter and up to one of the men on the other side. "Mr. Dent, let me help you with that tray, sir," he said, taking the tray from a man Charlie guessed to be in his seventies.

"Joe Dent," Marie said, gently pushing Charlie up to the counter.

Charlie scooped a spoonful of grits onto an awaiting plate. "Here—here you go," she said in a near whisper to a woman who couldn't quite meet her eyes.

"John likes to call them Mister and Miss or Mrs.," Marie continued. "He says it gives them a sense of pride. Respect."

Charlie scooped another spoonful, then another.

"Let me know if you need anything," Marie said, after making sure Charlie knew how to scoop grits. "Or your dad, of course."

Marie followed John's path around the counter. As Charlie scooped and muttered greetings—"Good morning" or "Enjoy!"—she kept a watch on them both as they moved around the dining room cluttered with wooden picnic tables covered in plastic tablecloths boasting large poinsettia blossoms.

John seemed sincere in the way he spoke to the men and women in the room. They both did. As though they worked as a team of one rather than two.

Charlie's insides fluttered, and she wondered . . .

⎯⎯∞⎯⎯

"Thanks for helping out," John said to her an hour later as he escorted her into his office. "Have a seat. Let's talk a minute."

Marie came in behind them carrying two cups of steaming coffee. "I don't know how you like it, Charlie," she said, placing the mugs on the desk.

"Oh—uh—cream and sugar."

Marie smiled. "Be right back then." She pushed a cup of black coffee toward John. "Here. Drink before you get cranky."

John smiled as she left the room and nodded toward the open door. "She takes care of me."

"Are you—do you two—?"

"Date?" He sat in his chair and brought the coffee to his lips, inhaling. "She makes the best coffee, I'll give her that." He took a long sip. "Yeah, I guess you could say we date. She was working here when I got here and we... I don't know. She's pretty special."

Charlie took in a shaky breath. "Does she know?"

John's brow rose. "About me? My past?"

Charlie nodded as Marie shot into the room carrying a small carton of milk, a few packets of sugar, and a spoon. "Here you go, Charlie." She placed the items on the desk near Charlie's chair. "Whole milk okay?"

"Perfect," Charlie lied.

Marie looked at John. "I'm going to help finish up in the kitchen. If you need me..."

"Thanks, Marie," he said, his voice quiet.

Charlie inhaled deeply as she tore into a packet of sugar. That voice. He spoke to Marie in the same tone he'd once used when speaking to her mother. To Gayle. *Before* their words had been fueled by drugs and desperation.

"Dad," Charlie asked, adding the milk. "Does she?"

"Yes," he said, taking another sip. "She knows. And I know all about hers as well."

Charlie's eyes shot to the door leading to the hallway. "Hers?"

"Sometimes, Charlie, you have to get down on the floor to understand what it's like to be there."

"Like Dickens. He supported the impoverished after his childhood experiences." She stirred the coffee until it turned creamy.

"That's what I mean. Dickens understood. You've had your issues—your mom and me, for example—but you've always lived in comfort. You've always had food on your table. You've never worn hand-me-down clothes that are tattered at best." He glanced down the hallway. "You didn't see them because the children are already in school where they get a hot meal provided by the government, but a few of those men and women you served aren't homeless on their own. They are heads of families who are homeless, not because they *want* to be. Some have made wrong choices, and some have had wrong choices made for them." He placed his mug on the desk. "There are times I feel like I'm no more than a drop of water in the ocean. Other times I feel like, maybe, I'm *doing something*. You know?" His eyes welled with tears. "Something that makes them feel less like a number and more like a human being."

Charlie swallowed past the lump in her throat. "Dad." She pinched her nose to keep it from stinging as she blinked back her own tears. One loan escapee darted down her cheek. "Tell me about Mr. Dent."

"Joe Dent," he said, leaning back in his chair. "A good man who started drinking to help with the anxiety as his business went under in the 2008 crash. Lost it, plus his home. His wife and his kids left him and went to live with her parents. After being in and out of jail from Florida to Tennessee—mostly for vagrancy and petty theft—he found his way here. I think I may have found a job for him—something that won't overwhelm him right off the bat—which is a real step."

"A job? He's too old, isn't he? Shouldn't he be on Social Security or something? Didn't he have retirement when his business went under?"

"Joe? Joe's fifty-five years old, sweetheart. If I can give him at least one good decade before Social Security kicks in, I will have done my job."

Marie's head jutted into the room. "Hey," she said, looking directly at John, concern shadowing her face. "Ivan the Terrible is here."

Charlie glanced from Marie to her father. He rubbed his forehead and took in a deep breath. "Did he say what he wanted?"

"You."

John exhaled slowly. "Send him back." He looked at Charlie.

"Charlie?" Marie said, as if on cue. "Would you like to come with me while your dad has this meeting?"

Charlie studied her father. Clearly this *Ivan* wasn't someone John wanted to see.

Shrewd as a snake. Innocent as a dove.

She stood. "Sure." Charlie picked up her coffee mug.

Halfway down the hall she passed a man who appeared to be in his forties. Broad shouldered. Stocky around the middle, as if he'd eaten one too many éclairs.

"Hi," he said, as pleasant as anything.

"Hello," she said back, keeping her voice firm, hoping she sounded like Sis when Sis wasn't happy with the way the day was turning out. Like *I'm watching you. I've memorized your face. So if my father suddenly comes up missing . . .*

She shook her head. She'd obviously watched one too many *Dateline* mysteries.

She stopped, ready to return to her father's office, as Marie said, "Would you like to see the new window boxes some of our men have made for the front windows?"

"I'm sorry, the what?"

"Some of the men made them, and the women painted them. When spring comes, the children are going to plant flowers in them. Spruce up the outside."

Charlie sighed. "Sure." She added a smile. "Of course." She followed Marie to the front and toward the front door and the sidewalk beyond. But her mind wasn't on window boxes. Instead, she was already planning how she'd manage to get back to her father's office.

And perhaps to the truth about who John Dixon really was.

16

Much they saw, and far they went, and many homes
they visited, but always with a happy end. The
Spirit stood beside sick-beds, and they were cheer-
ful; on foreign lands, and they were close at home;
by struggling men, and they were patient in their
greater hope; by poverty, and it was rich. In alms-
house, hospital, and jail, in misery's every refuge,
where vain man in his little brief authority had not
made fast the door, and barred the Spirit out, he left
his blessing, and taught Scrooge his precepts.

I knew it," Charlie said from her seat in the auditorium where she'd met Dusty a half hour before the others were to arrive. "I *told* you John Dixon hadn't changed." She dropped her head in her hand. "This is going to *kill* Sis."

"Okay," Dusty said, touching her hand with his own. "First of all, calm down."

Charlie's head shot up. "All of a sudden, I'm supposed to go look at window boxes while this *Ivan the Terrible*—not that I believe for a minute that's his name, Dusty, but obviously, he's . . . he's something—someone—hush-hush."

Dusty raised a brow as his hands came up, palms down. "Calm. Down."

"Oh, believe me, Dusty. I'm calm. You should have seen me during the drive home. I ranted and raved at God, at *John*, and even at Sis for allowing him back into our lives. But now? I'm *calm*."

"Okay. You're calm, or some odd impersonation of it. Now tell me again *exactly* what you heard." His eyes held hers. "No embellishment."

"I don't embellish."

"All southerners embellish. It's in our DNA."

"This is no time for humor, even if it's true." She took a deep breath. Exhaled. "Okay. After I saw the window boxes, I told Marie I was going to the bathroom, which is off from the storage room. But instead I went down the hall. I figured

143

if anyone asked what I was doing, I'd say I needed my purse, which was in Da—John's office."

"All right."

"That's when I heard him—John—say, 'I told you I'd get it for you, and I will. I also told you that you'd have to wait until after the play in Testament. *That's* when I'll have it.' I know he means money, Dusty. He's going to take the money from the play to pay off some kind of, I don't know, some kind of gambling debt or drug deal."

Dusty shook his head. "Where do you get this stuff, Miss Drama?"

Fury shook Charlie as searing heat rose within her. "I realize, Dusty, that maybe I've watched one too many crime dramas, so maybe I'm being all Miss Drama and a little too quick to judge—"

"A little?"

"But you don't know him like I do."

He raised his hands. "Okay, okay, okay. You're right. I don't. So then what do you propose to do?"

Charlie sank into the hardness of the seat. "That's just it. I don't know. If I tell Sis, she'll be hurt *and* mad with me. She'll defend him for sure. She surely won't consider anything but the best about him. But if I'm right and I confront him, then he'll pooh-pooh it away and come up with another explanation and plan, which means he'll keep on fooling Sis and she'll get hurt eventually anyway."

"Hmm. Now you're thinking logically. And truthfully."

"The only thing I know to do is—and this is where you come in—"

"Me?"

"Yes. You have to ask for an accounting of the money once he gets it."

"Why would *I* ask for an accounting?"

"It's *your* show, isn't it?"

"Charlie, I'm just the director. The school's drama teacher. The ones who'd have to ask for an accounting are the school board members, and I'm not sure they're going to ask until after the show when the final sales are in. Especially not without causing suspicion." His eyes widened. "I mean, on the off chance that you're right."

"I *am* right, Dusty. And you don't know for sure. They might."

"They won't."

Charlie glanced at her watch. "The kids and carolers will be here shortly." She sighed. "Meanwhile, we have two weeks to figure this thing out."

"We?"

Charlie frowned. "Oh, all right. Me."

Dusty grinned. "Grammatically incorrect," he teased. "*I* have two weeks, not me have two weeks. You being a teacher and all, I think you owe it to yourself to keep your grammar in check. May help with the job search. How's that going, by the way?"

She sneered. "Never you mind." Charlie stood. "I'm going to the music room to wait on the carolers. Mr. Hartselle is having problems with 'I Saw a Maiden,' and I promised to meet him a few minutes early."

Charlie met Ashlynne for lunch on Tuesday and recounted her story. "I know you're a research hound," she said when Ashlynne's eyes grew wide, and Charlie knew she needed to get to the point of their lunch. "And I'm wondering what you can tell me about this Ivan person. Or my father."

Ashlynne nodded as she bit into a dill spear. "Okay," she said around the crunch. She chewed a moment longer, then swallowed before continuing. "A journalist learns never to presume guilt or innocence, so let me tell you straight up that I'm not necessarily convinced your father is hiding anything."

Charlie started to take another bite of her sandwich, then set it back on the plate. "But what about what I heard? He said, 'I told you I'd get it for you, and I will.' And 'I also told you that you'd have to wait until after the play in Testament. *That's* when I'll have it.' Have *what* is the question." She reached for the sandwich again, this time biting into it fully.

"And you think this is some kind of drug deal."

Charlie nodded. "Or gambling," she said around the food, then swallowed. "I think whoever this Ivan is, that's his real name and Marie just calls him 'the Terrible.' You know...like..."

"I know, but what if it's not? Or what if *your father's* not?"

"Not what?"

"In over his head with gambling or drug debts? Whether Ivan is his real name or not, and he is—I don't know—the landlord of the building and John is behind on the rent? What if he needs the money from the play to simply *make rent*, Charlie?"

Charlie shook her head as she swallowed and reached for the large glass of water on the table in front of her. "No, no, no," she mumbled, then took a long swig from the bendy straw. "You don't know him like I do." She returned the glass to the table. "Look, this isn't a Hallmark movie where all turns out right in the end and everyone is saying, 'God bless us, every one.'" She sighed. "Besides, John Dickens never really changed, and neither has John Dixon."

Ashlynne cocked a brow. "I'm sorry, what?"

"Never mind." She clasped her hands together as though pleading. "Please? Will you look into it? Use all your investigative abilities?"

Ashlynne nodded. "All right, Charlie. Okay. I haven't had a good story to dig into for a long time anyway so, yeah. I'll let you know something soon."

⸻

"Any bites on a new job?" Sis asked on Friday evening from her side of the kitchen table, where she tied blue bows on small gold-foiled gift bags.

"Not really," Charlie said. She picked up a sheet of silver tissue paper to wrap another of the thirty-some-odd *A Christmas Carol* commemorative ornaments Dusty planned to give the actors and carolers on the evening of dress rehearsal. "Actually, that would require *looking* for a job or *applying* for a job." She nestled the ornament within the paper and set it into one of the gift bags, then handed it to her grandmother for the final garnishment.

Sis glanced up. "You haven't even looked? Not once?"

Charlie shrugged. "I don't know, Sis. I go online and start the search, and then I get distracted. Besides, with the last few days being a frenzy of rehearsals and rounding up these ornaments for Dusty—"

"And going out for coffee after rehearsals *with* Dusty."

"Sis."

Sis slid the ribbon between the handles. "So what do you think the distractions are about?"

"I don't know, really. I just can't seem to concentrate on too much." Charlie swallowed past the half-truth. She knew exactly where the problem lay. First, seeing Dusty again. Then, being roped into working on a play she'd not been even remotely excited about. Seeing her father again and all that went with that.

And him.

Now, she was worried that Sis would be hurt by his reentry into their lives. She looked up at Sis and, seeing the concern on her face, forced herself to brighten. "Don't worry, Sis," she said. "I'm sure whatever is holding me back will be over once Christmas has come and gone."

"Maybe," Sis said, raising a brow, "subconsciously, you want to stay here. Close to Dustin."

Maybe. Or maybe God planned all along that she'd be here when the bottom dropped out and Sis learned the truth about her son. *Maybe.* If only Ashlynne would call with news. Perhaps then she could stop John from damaging his relationship with Sis any further. The possibility of Sis never having to hear of this gave her renewed hope.

But Ashlynne needed to let her know something. She glanced at the calendar. Three full days had gone by. Four since she'd seen her father. Only eleven until the play.

How hard could it be to look up this Ivan, for pity's sake?

17

———

"I was only going to say," said Scrooge's nephew,
"that the consequence of his taking a dislike to
us, and not making merry with us, is, as I think,
that he loses some pleasant moments, which could
do him no harm. I am sure he loses pleasanter
companions than he can find in his own thoughts,
either in his mouldy old office, or his dusty cham-
bers. I mean to give him the same chance every
year, whether he likes it or not, for I pity him. He
may rail at Christmas till he dies, but he can't help
thinking better of it—I defy him—if he finds me
going there, in good temper, year after year, and
saying Uncle Scrooge, how are you?"

John brought Marie to church on Sunday. Although Charlie tried to concentrate on the pastor's message, she could only replay the events of the previous Monday.

One thing was certain: Marie *knew* the truth about John.

She shook her head before realizing what she'd done, and she quickly looked down to the opened Bible in her lap. The words blurred as she forced herself to think through the evidence. Marie knew about John's past. He knew about hers. Which only meant they were thick as thieves. Marie also knew about the man she'd called "Ivan the Terrible"— enough so that she'd whisked Charlie out of the office when he'd arrived to talk to John.

Charlie looked up, hoping she could focus on the pastor's words. Instead, she caught Ashlynne looking at her from across the center aisle of the church. Ashlynne's pretty eyes widened as she mouthed, "We need to talk."

Charlie's breath caught in her throat and she nodded. A quick look at her watch told her they had at least another ten minutes before the service would come to a close.

Ten minutes. May as well be ten days.

Ashlynne looped her arm with Charlie's as soon as they exited the church, and she steered her toward the side of the building. "Will," she said to her husband, who walked beside them. "My back is killing me. Do you mind getting the car and picking me up here?"

Charlie watched as concern crossed his face. He placed his hand on the small of her back, which bowed under the weight of their unborn child. "You okay?" He looked to her belly and back to her face.

She nodded and smiled easily. "I'm fine. A little tired is all, and I don't want to walk that far."

When he moved out of earshot, Charlie turned her full attention to Ashlynne. "Are you *really* tired? I don't want to think you've *lied* for me." She looked over to the brick structure beside them. "Especially not five minutes after we leave the house of God."

Ashlynne shook her head. "Truth is, I'm not a little tired. I'm *very* tired." She peered down. "And look at my feet. From what I can see, they look like puff balls."

Charlie did. "Honestly." She smiled. "And I'm curious. Did you know you're wearing similar shoes but of a different color?"

Ashlynne sighed as she placed a hand on Charlie's arm for balance, then stuck one foot out and then the other. "I'm going to shoot Will Decker when we get home," she said. "And he better not claim to be color-blind."

Charlie giggled. "Okay, okay." She looked toward the parking lot. "Dead man driving will be back in a minute. So? What did you find out?"

"Your father went to prison in 1998."

"I know *that*. Tell me something I *don't* know."

Ashlynne took Charlie's hand and squeezed. "Let me do this my way." She looked over her shoulder. "And by the way, your grandmother is over there trying to look casual as she stares at us."

"Great," Charlie breathed out.

"Okay. He was released in 2003, early for good behavior." She knew that, too.

"In 2005, he returned to prison and served eight years. When he was released, he went to a halfway house in West Virginia where he lived for six months. While there, he took a job in a shelter—"

"*Ashlynne*. I know all this. What do you know about this *Ivan* person?" She air quoted the name.

Ashlynne sighed as a car pulled up near the curb. "There's Will." She blinked. "To answer your question—nothing. There is absolutely zilch linking your father to anyone named Ivan. I've checked the prison records. No Ivan served while your father was there. I've checked the halfway house. Nothing. And to answer your next question, the shelter in Morganton is owned by a man named David Herbick." She waved at William, letting him know she saw him. "Walk me to my car."

Charlie did. "Did you find out anything on David Herbick? Like what he looks like because I got a good look at this man when we passed each other in the hall."

Ashlynne kept her eyes on the ground in front of her. "Not really. I pulled up an images search, but all I got was a bunch of strangers' faces and a few of David Beckham."

"David Beckham?"

"There's no accounting for Google. But as to what I know about David *Herbick*, to be honest, not much other than that he owns a good bit of the downtown area where the shelter is. He ran for city council once and lost." She stopped on the sidewalk. "But that was a few years ago, and there was no picture with the article other than one from a distance." She paused. "He was shaking the hand of the man who defeated him."

Will got out of the car and opened the passenger side door. "Hon?"

"Coming, sweetie. Give me one second." She turned back to Charlie. "He's been married to the same woman since right after high school. Three kids—all at NC State."

"A dead end then."

"Or," Ashlynne said, "maybe there is *nothing to find*. Remember what I said. We journalists don't see guilt or innocence until we've looked at the facts. If we can't find guilt, we have to presume innocence."

But Charlie shook her head. "No, Ash. There's something. Trust me. And one way or the other, I'm going to figure out what it is."

Ashlynne squeezed her hand once more. "My prayers are with you then." She started to take a step, then stopped. "Remember, Charlie, sometimes we open someone else's can of worms to our own detriment."

Charlie understood the words of warning. Years earlier, Ashlynne had uncovered dirt on the high school football coach, but she'd done so unethically and illegally. She'd been given a firm warning on top of a hefty fine, but that had been the least of her problems. The town of Testament had taken its own sweet time in offering forgiveness to her for revealing a harsh truth about its beloved citizen.

"Hmm," Charlie said. "Still, when you're right about someone, you're right about someone."

And Charlie had no doubt, when it came to John Dixon, she was one hundred percent right.

Sis met Charlie halfway back to the parking lot. "What were you two talking about?" she asked, turning back toward the cars. "It looked intense."

"Oh," Charlie said, her mind searching for an answer, "this and that."

"Well," Sis said, looking to where John, Marie, Dusty, and Jeremy stood in a semicircle, waiting on them. "I've asked everyone to come back to the house for lunch. I think the pot roast I put in the Crock-Pot will be enough to serve everyone, but I'm not sure about dessert."

Charlie sucked in her breath.

"I know," Sis said. "I knew your father was coming, but I hadn't counted on his new friend."

"*Girl*friend, Sis. They're *dating.*"

Sis stopped. "Does that bother you?"

"In a way. A little." She shook her head. "Not really, I just don't think of Dad as, you know, being romantic at *this* point in his life." Charlie looked back to the small group to see Dusty smiling at her. She returned the expression as a thought came to mind. "Hey, Sis? Do you mind if I ride back to the house with Dusty? We can stop at the grocery's bakery and pick up a pie."

Her grandmother winked. "I think that's a marvelous idea." Sis's face brightened. "And I think I'd like to spend a little time with Master Jeremy, so why don't I have him ride with me? That way you and Dusty can be alone."

Charlie rolled her eyes. "He has to sit in a car seat, Sis."

"Oh, pooh. Those things can be moved, can't they?"

Minutes later, Jeremy's car seat had been transferred from Dusty's car to Sis's, and everyone had gotten into the assigned automobiles. After a quick trip to the bakery, Charlie and Dusty headed back to the car. As soon as Dusty closed the driver's door and started the car, he said, "Okay. I'm sure you put Ashlynne up to some sort of investigative work. And I'm equally sure you're going to tell me about it."

Charlie frowned as she crossed her arms. "She came up with nothing. There's no Ivan to speak of—unless his name is really David—and everything Sis told me about my father is true."

"So then maybe your father is on the up-and-up, and there's nothing to be suspicious of?"

"*Dusty*," Charlie said, turning as best she could under the constraints of the seat belt. "I saw a man they called Ivan. I *heard* what my father said to him. *Something* is going on. Now, I have a question. Something that just dawned on me."

"Oh boy."

Charlie looked out the windshield.

"Dusty, how do folks buy their tickets to the play? Online or at the door?"

"Mostly online. At the door is cash only, assuming we have seating available."

"How many tickets have you sold so far?"

"Almost all of them. We might have twenty seats left." He looked her way. "Where are you going with this, Charlie?"

"How is the shelter in Morganton getting the funds?"

"It's being transferred into the shelter's account."

"When?"

"I don't know, honestly. That's not my role in this."

Charlie sighed. "But will they get it *before* or *after* the play?"

"Again. I don't know."

"Then who would?"

He shrugged. "Your grandmother, maybe." They pulled into the driveway. The family was still outside, having been delayed by Jeremy's fascination with some autumn leaves. "Charlie?"

"What?"

The car slowed to a stop. Dusty turned off the engine and then looked at her fully. "Why don't you stop all this? If Ashlynne can't find anything, then maybe there's nothing to be found." He unbuckled his seat belt, and Charlie did the same. "Or—and here's an idea for you—give this thing to God. Ask *Him* to reveal the unseen things. He knows the hearts of men, after all."

Charlie felt the wind ease out of her sails. "I want to, Dusty. And that all sounds good in theory. But what...what if I'm right? I don't want Sis to have to live in Testament—" She glanced out the window to see John staring at her, and she forced a smile. "I don't want Sis to have to live here after the storm dies down. If he steals all the money from these good people, well, she's risking more than I think she realizes." The family had gone inside, Jeremy holding Sis's hand. "Dusty, I lived in Testament with no one knowing the truth. And Sis never had to say a word. But *if I'm right*, then the one thing we've tried so hard to keep hidden will be exposed."

Dusty reached for the door handle. "Don't underestimate your grandmother, Charlie. I think she's a whole lot smarter than you give her credit for."

18

"Ghost of the Future! I fear you more than any spectre I have seen. But as I know your purpose is to do me good, and as I hope to live to be another man from what I was, I am prepared to bear you company.... Lead on! The night is waning fast, and it is precious time to me, I know. Lead on, Spirit!"

—*Ebenezer Scrooge*

A day or two later, Charlie put on a mantle of bravery and asked her grandmother outright about the money and how it would be accounted for. Sis had passed her off as easily as Dusty had, only with less suspicion.

By the time the morning of the eighteenth rolled in, Charlie had gone back to Morganton to volunteer three times, mainly in hopes that she could learn something more. Instead, everything about her father's work—his and Marie's—appeared to be more legitimate than ever.

The day before the play, after serving breakfast with Marie and the other girls, Charlie found her father in his office and came right out and asked him. "Dad? How will you get the money from the play's proceeds? I mean, once the play is over."

He stood on the opposite side of his desk, a manila file half open in his hands, and he looked up when she posed her question. "Why do you ask?"

She shrugged, sitting in the same chair she'd occupied when she'd first heard the name "Ivan the Terrible." The name that had changed everything, taking her from hopeful to doubtful. "I don't know. I just wondered, that's all."

John closed the file and placed it on his desk. "It's fairly simple, really. As people buy their tickets online, the money goes through an online service and is then—after a small fee is taken out—transferred to a special account for the shelter."

"So you actually have the money *now*."

"Technically, yes. But I've been asked not to use it until after the nineteenth. I guess it makes the accounting easier. I have to show how much came in—you know, the online money plus the cash from the evening of the play—and then, of course, I'll have to give a full report to the Department of Social Services."

His answer caught her off guard. "Really?"

He gave her a look of surprise. "Well, of course, Charlie. We're regulated here. What'd you think?"

But before Charlie could answer, Marie stepped in. "Problem."

"What's that?"

"Arleen just called. She's not going to be able to come in today."

John sighed heavily. "We'll get through it."

"Who's Arleen?" Charlie asked.

Marie stepped fully into the room. "Our after-school tutor. Most of the children here are behind on their subjects, so . . ."

Charlie sat up straight. "Can I help?" She looked from John to Marie and back to her father again. "I'm a teacher. I can fill in."

John nodded. "Sure." He seemed pleased. "Thank you, Charlie."

That afternoon John introduced her to the dozen or so children—a decent blend of boys and girls, most of them under the age of twelve—as their new teacher but not as his daughter. "Best they not know that quite yet," he mumbled to her before leaving the room.

162

"All right, kids," Charlie said to the anxious faces, all of them so precious, she could hardly bear to think they were homeless.

Or that she could have been one of them had it not been for Sis.

"Take your seats, take out your schoolwork, and I'm going to come around and see where you need help most."

An hour later she had the younger children sitting in what she called "Story Time Circle." She wanted the older children to have additional quiet time to finish up their homework, and this arrangement allowed for that.

"Mason," she said to one of the boys, "why don't you go pick out a book from the shelf over there," she said glancing at the hodgepodge of library castoffs.

"Yes, Miss Dixon." The boy, who appeared to be ten in stature but forty by the wisdom in his eyes, swiveled out of his chair and ambled over to the bookcase.

Charlie felt a tug on the sleeve of her sweater. She looked down to the angelic black eyes of a little girl who'd introduced herself earlier as Tamika. "Yes?"

"If *your* name is Miss Dixon and the man who runs this place is *Mister* Dixon, does that make him your husband?"

Charlie opened her mouth to protest, then closed it and opened it again as one of the other children said, "He's too old to be her husband."

"Actually," Charlie said, "you're right. He's not my husband. I'm not married."

"Then is he your daddy?" another child asked.

Charlie raised her chin, unsure how to answer. "Mmm...yes," she said, settling on the truth. "Mr. Dixon *is* my father."

Tamika tugged again on her sweater. "You're lucky," she said as Mason returned with a worn copy of *Matilda* and handed it to her.

"Thank you, Mason," she said to him, then looked again at Tamika. "I am? Why's that?"

"Because you got a daddy," she said. "And he's real nice."

Charlie swallowed hard as her breath caught in her throat. "Yes," she said. "I guess so."

The nineteenth came in a flurry of a new cold front, costume fittings, and last-minute set changes. As the day went on, the temperature dropped outside while the auditorium echoed with Dusty singing, "It's Beginning to Look a Lot Like Christmas."

With every start of the song, someone else—a few of the teens in the show or one of the stagehands—sang back, "Everywhere you go!"

At five o'clock, within a whirlwind of makeup and costumes, Dusty jutted his head out the back stage door and then peered over his shoulder to where Charlie stood with a handful of sheet music for the night's performance. "Hey," he said, "come look."

She stepped behind him to look over his shoulder. "Snow," she whispered.

"It's like ole Charles himself is providing a Dickens Christmas for us."

Charlie grinned at him. "The Ghost of Christmas Present?"

Dusty returned his gaze to the outside where large flakes fell at an angle to gather atop the trash bin and black asphalt. "It's coming down pretty hard already." He pulled his phone from his jeans pocket, pressed an app, and studied it.

"Weather Channel says we're in for a few inches before the night's over."

Charlie kissed his cheek and started back. "Well, you got your wish, Mr. Kennedy. A Dickens Christmas outside and a Dickens Christmas inside."

Sis, John, and Marie arrived an hour later, their hands full of after-the-show reception food and drink, and their coats thickly dusted in melting snow. "It must be really coming down out there," Charlie said, taking a tray of homemade peppermint bark from Sis.

"I've never seen it like this," she commented, then pointed to one of the white linen-covered tables they'd set aside for the after-party. "Let's put the sweet stuff on this table, drinks over there. John, go ahead and put the coffeemaker at that end of the table."

Her son did as he was told while Marie held up a slow cooker that emitted a delicious aroma. "Where should I put this?"

Sis pointed. "There." She looked at Charlie and Dusty. "I know you two are busy. Go about your work. We'll get all this set up."

Charlie kissed her grandmother's cheek. "Don't get too cold going in and out."

Sis brushed her aside. "You act like I'm an old woman."

"Never." She turned to see her father placing the commercial-sized coffeemaker on the table, then he stopped to stare at it. He visibly took a deep breath and exhaled.

"Um . . . Dad?"

He turned to look at her, his face relaxing.

Charlie walked to him. "You okay?"

John's brow furrowed. "Yeah. Of course." He smiled. "A little stressed. It's been a long week."

She blinked. "It's Tuesday."

He chuckled. "In my line of work, Charlie, one day pretty much runs into another."

Marie joined them, her expression anxious. "Anything else I can do?"

Charlie took a step back. "Um…you know…ask Sis," she said, pointing to her grandmother. She held up the sheet music. "I need to get to my singers."

Charlie walked out of the room and down a narrow hallway, her mind racing and her heart sure the two of them—John and Marie—were planning something.

Exactly *what*, she still wasn't sure. And all the evidence was stacked up *against* proving that. The staff at the shelter loved them, the children adored them, the adults respected and praised them.

And so far the dish hadn't run off with the spoon, although one looked anxious and the other stressed.

But…still.

Charlie mentally kicked herself. Why couldn't she simply let go of her doubts and trust John Dixon? Why couldn't she be more like Sis? Or Charles Dickens?

"Miss Dixon?"

Charlie stopped at the sound of the voice behind her and turned to see Gwen Brower standing in full costume. "Look at *you*," she breathed out.

Gwen bridged the gap between them. "Have you ever seen anything so beautiful?" She turned, then curtseyed, which brought a laugh from Charlie.

"You're playing the part of Fred's beautiful wife." Charlie lifted Gwen's chin with her fingertips. "Head up. Remember, you're genteel. You're society. You're lovely."

Gwen blushed. "Wearing your gloves over these past couple of weeks has prepped me a little," she said. "Did you know both my parents are going to be here tonight? They left my brothers and sisters working the tree farm so they could come."

"I'm so glad to hear that. I'm sure they'll be proud." She smiled. "And by the way—they're not *my* gloves. They're *your* gloves."

"Yes, ma'am."

Charlie glanced at her watch. "Go practice your lines. In one hour, this place will be full of people, and all our hard work will finally come down to the moment."

"Showtime."

"Showtime." Charlie laid her hand over Gwen's lace-gloved hands. "Break a leg."

Gwen's laughter rang out like a church bell. "Yes, ma'am," she said as she turned back toward the girls' dressing room.

19

———∞———

"I will honour Christmas in my heart, and try
to keep it all the year. I will live in the Past, the
Present, and the Future! The Spirits of all Three
shall strive within me. I will not shut out the lessons that they teach."

—*Ebenezer Scrooge*

When the last line of the play had been spoken, the last note of Charlie's contemporary version of "God Rest Ye Merry, Gentlemen" had been sung, hugs and kisses under the mistletoe had been passed around, and the last of the food and drink had been consumed at the after-party, Charlie collapsed in a chair that had been left in one corner of the room.

Dusty, finding his own chair and carrying it over, joined her. "I could curl up on the floor over there right now and go immediately to sleep."

Charlie blinked long and slow, turning her head to look at him before dropping it to his shoulder. "Oh, no. You're my pillow."

Dusty's head rested against the wall. "Ha ha ha."

She yawned. "Ho ho ho." Then slanting her eyes up, she added, "Where's Jeremy?"

"Mom and Dad's. He was sound asleep in Dad's arms before act two."

"Mm."

Dusty wiggled his shoulder. "Up with you. You, my dear, still have some explaining to do. I clearly do *not* remember hearing 'God Rest Ye Merry,' sung in such an arrangement during rehearsals."

Charlie giggled. "*Shenanigans*," she said, remembering Clara Pressley's words.

"I have no idea what that means."

"It means revenge is kinda sweet."

He tilted her face up and kissed her. "Speaking of *sweet.*"

She sighed, then looked out over the mess in the room. "I vote for cleaning this up tomorrow after school."

He cocked a brow. "I vote for *you* cleaning this up in the morning while *I* work."

Charlie stretched, then allowed her shoulders to sag. "Oh, that's right. I'm working in Morganton tomorrow afternoon." She stood and Dusty followed her.

"In the afternoon?"

"Yeah," she said as they walked out of the room, grabbing their coats and gloves near the door. "I forgot to tell you. The after-school tutor had something come up yesterday so I stayed and helped out. I thought it was for one day only, but before I left, John got an e-mail with her resignation. She'd found a better-paying job starting after the first of the year, and she said she needed the time between now and Christmas to get ready for it." Charlie conveniently left off the details of Tamika's praises of John.

Dusty switched off the light. "And you volunteered?"

They continued down the half-lit hallway toward the back door. "I did. I enjoyed it really. I told John I'd fill in until the holidays." She stopped and sighed. "I know you don't want to hear this, but Da—John acted a little funny tonight and—"

Dusty turned to face her. "Are you starting that again?"

"Hear me out. Even Marie acted weird. I'm telling you, they're up to something."

Dusty opened the outside door and looked out at the thick shroud of snow. "Would you look at that?"

An idea came to mind, formed on the skirts of a memory from childhood. Seventh grade. Snow shutting the school down. All the kids gathering at the Deckers' house to drink hot chocolate and make snow angels and snowmen. She'd so wanted Dusty to make an angel with her—side by side—a temporary forever. But he'd been more interested in the snowball fight behind the house.

"Hey," she said slowly. "Wanna make snow angels in the parking lot?"

"You mean like we're kids?"

"Yeah. Remember childhood? When life seemed simple and—"

"You're nuts, woman." Dusty pointed before Charlie could retort. "I'm parked down there. Where are you?"

She stood on the platform and stared at Dusty's lone car at the far corner of the building. "On the other side. Not too far from you." Awkwardness filled the air—dark and wet. Charlie didn't want the evening to end, especially as wonderful as it had been for everyone. She brought her eyes to Dusty's. "Want to come by the house? Sis is sure to have some of her world-famous cocoa on the stove when we get there." Her words filled the night with hope.

But Dusty shook his head. "I don't know, Charlie. I'm really tired."

She slid her arms around his waist and smiled up at him. "Please?"

He chuckled. "All right. For one cup."

She reached up and kissed his chin. "Follow me then?"

He looped her arm with his. "No. You ride with me. The roads are slippery, and you've not driven on anything like this in a long time."

That much was true. "What about my car?"

"I'll make sure you get it tomorrow." He tugged her along. "Come on now. I can already taste that cocoa."

Tired as they were, both Charlie and Dusty sang carols and laughed at the top of their lungs for the majority of the drive. When they reached Sis's cottage, Dusty parked next to Sis's car, and they paused, looking at the porch rails strung with lighted garland. "You should have called to let her know I was coming."

Charlie unbuckled her seat belt, then faced him. "Don't worry. Sis loves you."

He reached over, cupping her face in his leather-gloved hands and brought his lips sweetly to hers. "And do you?"

Taken aback, Charlie forced herself to breathe. "What?" she whispered.

"Love me? Because I have to tell you, Charlie, I think you're nuts in this obsession about your father, but putting that aside, I . . . well, I haven't felt this way in a long, long time." He held her eyes with his own. "I mean it. I never thought—after Emily—that I could . . . that I would . . ."

She kissed him again. "I've loved you, Dusty, since we were kids. Remember?"

"No," he said, shaking his head. "You loved the *idea* of me." His eyes widened. "But do you love *me*? Now?"

She nodded. "I think so, yes. But, well—you're supposed to say it first."

"I love you," his words rushed out.

"I love you, too."

They both laughed.

He looked out the window and furrowed his brow. "I thought—"

Charlie sat back. "What?"

"I thought I heard your dad say he was coming here—him and Marie—to spend a few minutes with your grandmother."

"When did he say that?"

"I heard him right before they left."

She looked at her watch. "Well, maybe they've come and gone. We were at the school a lot longer than everyone else."

"True." He shook his head with a laugh. "Oh, no."

"What?"

"I'm starting to sound like you. All suspicion and doubt." Charlie laughed with him. "Let's go in."

Charlie knocked on the door as they entered. "Sis?" she called out, inhaling, hoping for the aroma of cocoa simmering on the stove and smelling nothing but the cinnamon broom hanging on the door between the breakfast nook and the living room.

Sis hurried toward them from the living room. "Have you seen John?" she asked, her voice pitched.

"No." Charlie looked at Dusty and felt her lips pull tight.

"He didn't come here after the play?" Dusty asked.

"No. And he said he'd be right here." Sis wrung her hands. "I don't understand this."

Charlie shrugged out of her coat and set her purse on the table. "Okay," she said, her insides twisting. "Let's not panic too quickly. Did you try to call his cell?"

Sis ran fingers through her white bob, pushing it away from her face. "No." Her eyes looked wild and troubled. "I didn't even think—"

Dusty took Charlie's coat and, adding his own, laid them over one of the kitchen chairs as Charlie pulled her iPhone from her purse. She dialed the number and waited, then dropped the phone from her ear.

Dusty walked into the living room. "It's ringing in here—"

Charlie and Sis followed behind him to see the lit face of John's phone, which lay in the far left corner of the leather sofa. Sis rushed over to pick it up and turn it off. "It must have fallen out of his pocket when they came by earlier. He sat here while I finished up."

Worry and anger blended inside of Charlie, stirring like the whirling dust of snow she could see in the moonlight beyond the French doors. "What has he done?"

"What?" Sis asked, as though she hadn't heard.

Charlie shook her head. "Does he have a home phone?"

Sis nodded. "I have the number written down in my book." She quickly returned with the small blue address book she'd recorded numbers in for as long as Charlie could remember. She dialed the number from her own cell phone. After a few seconds, she ended the call. "I got a recording saying the lines are down."

Dusty walked over to the French doors and peered out. "I'm not surprised. We're not used to storms like this." He turned back to the room. "Up north, maybe, but not here."

Sis tossed the address book onto an end table and crossed her arms. "I'm so worried."

Charlie raked her teeth over her bottom lip. "I cannot believe he'd do this. Wait. Yes, I can." She focused all of her attention on Dusty. "Didn't I tell you he was up to something?"

"What are you talking about?" Sis asked.

"I—Sis—I didn't want you to know." She paused. "That first day I worked for Dad, I overheard something." Her vision blurred with tears, matching her grandmother's.

"Charlie Dixon. *What* are you telling me?"

Dusty came up beside Sis and helped her sit. "Look, Mrs. Dixon, I . . . I'm not one to jump to conclusions, and I've argued all the way with Charlie about this." Sis's eyes penetrated his as he explained about the man named "Ivan" who had come to the shelter, concluding with Charlie's suspicions. "Now," he said with a sigh, "this whole thing could be explained any number of ways. One, he *could* have taken off somehow with the money, or two, he—"

Sis jumped up. "Is that what you think?" she demanded of Charlie. "You think John has run off with the money from tonight's show?"

Charlie crossed the room, reaching for her grandmother's hands.

Sis pulled back. "No," she said. "I can't believe this. I cannot believe you would have kept all this from me—first of all. And second, *why* didn't you just ask John about this Ivan person?"

"Sis, please—" Charlie felt her insides go numb. She couldn't lose Sis. Not to this. And certainly not to her father's schemes. It would be too much.

"No, Charlie. Answer the question."

"Which is?"

"Why didn't you ask John?"

"Because I...because...Sis, how would I know he was telling the truth?"

Sis pointed her finger at Charlie's nose. "Sometimes, Charlie, you simply have to have a little *faith*." She squeezed her index finger and thumb together. "All you need is a modicum."

"A mustard seed's worth," Dusty supplied.

Charlie shot him her best "you're not helping" look. At least, she hoped it was. "You mean like you did, Sis?"

Sis crossed her arms again. "What are you talking about now, Charlene?"

Charlie placed her hands on her hips and looked down, counting to five as she did so. "I'm talking about," she began, her eyes finding her grandmother's again, "I'm telling you that I *know*."

20

—❧—

"I am as light as a feather, I am as happy as an angel, I am as merry as a schoolboy. I am as giddy as a drunken man. A merry Christmas to everybody! A happy New Year to all the world!"

—*Ebenezer Scrooge*

You know *what?*"

Charlie pointed to the chair her grandmother had been in only a moment before. "Can we sit? Please?"

Sis went to her favorite chair instead while Dusty took one end of the sofa and Charlie took the other.

"Sis, I overheard you one night when I was a child, telling Dad that you didn't care if he'd gone to Bible study and church every single day—or something to that effect—you were not going to relinquish me to him. Do you remember that?"

Sis pinked. "Of course I do. But that has nothing to do with a lack of faith in my son."

"Doesn't it? If you trusted that he'd changed, wouldn't you have—at the very least—asked him to come here? To live with us?"

"Don't be ridiculous, Charlie. People would have talked, especially with Gayle still in jail."

Charlie bent forward, clasping her hands. "Is that the only reason, Sis? Be honest. Please."

Sis studied the fire before answering. "No. Of course not. I wanted you to have the most normal childhood possible. And I wanted him to prove himself." Her face turned back to Charlie and Dusty. "I believe with my whole heart that he has. He's doing wonderful things over at the shelter, even bringing our two counties together. Did you know he's planning to open a shelter here once he gets this one fully operational?"

"No," Charlie said, her voice quiet. "I didn't know that."

"Did you also know that he's been planning to ask you to take over the tutoring—full time—and to help him develop a truly functioning educational department for both shelters?"

"What?" *Then how could he—*

Dusty sighed. "I think, ladies, the real questions right *now* are, where is he and is there any way to check and see if the money has been taken?"

Sis's eyes widened. "There is."

"There is?" Charlie asked.

"Yes. I have all the information from the online service to the bank." She shot a look at Charlie. "My son gave it to me."

"Sis—"

Her grandmother stood. "I'll be right back," she said, then headed down the hallway toward the bedrooms.

"Oh my gosh," Charlie said. "She's so angry with me."

Dusty shook his head. "Do you blame her?"

"I *know* I'm right, Dusty. If she can get into that account, I guarantee you it's been drained."

Sis returned, her footsteps heavy, carrying her laptop and a sliver of lavender paper. "I wrote it on this Post-it note." She sat again and opened her laptop. As it booted up, Dusty and Charlie moved to stand behind the rocker.

"You'll see," Sis said.

Charlie shook her head, saddened even further by her grandmother's refusal to at least entertain the truth.

A minute later, Sis said, "Here we go." Charlie closed her eyes, afraid of what she'd see. If she were right, the victory would be a bitter one. If she were wrong, she had hammered a nail in a coffin designed only to bury the priceless relationship she had with her grandmother.

"Told you," Sis said.

"It's there," Dusty confirmed.

Charlie opened her eyes. She blinked, then bent her knees for a better look. "I don't know what to say—I..." She stood, went around to the front of the chair, and squatted again while a line from Dickens's classic ran through her mind as if it were her favorite story of all time—*Best and happiest of all, the Time before him was his own, to make amends in!* "Sis, I'm sorry." Her hand pressed against her abdomen; she felt as though she'd been kicked in the gut. "I was so sure."

Dusty sighed. "This only tells us that John didn't run off with the money. It doesn't tell us where he is."

Sis's eyes filled with tears. "While you've been worried about the money, I've been worried about my son lying in a ditch somewhere."

Charlie placed both hands on Sis's knees. "Sis," she whispered, "I'm sure he's okay."

Her grandmother's brow rose. "Like you were so sure he'd stolen the money."

Pain shot through her, rising up from beyond that evening. Beyond the past few weeks. Hurt at what felt like a lifetime of rejection and confusion surfaced, bringing with it further uncertainty. If John wasn't the scoundrel she'd so readily believed, then perhaps he *had* become the father she'd once known and loved. He'd become her daddy again.

And maybe all he was asking for, beyond another chance, was..."Forgive me, Sis. Please. I'm so, so sorry." A tear slipped down her cheek.

Sis's hands cupped Charlie's chin, and her thumb brushed away the tear. "Of course you're forgiven, Charlie. But this forgiveness thing goes both ways. We are forgiven *in the same way* as we forgive. *You* have to somehow find a way to reconcile all this with your father."

"Like by *asking...*" Dusty pulled his phone out of his pocket, and Charlie stood, her hand slipping into her grandmother's.

"What are you doing?"

"Calling the sheriff's office. Maybe there's been an accident reported." He shook his head. "Although I don't know how. We surely would have seen it."

"Come to think of it, the only vehicle I saw in town," Charlie added, "was the Browers' truck. But we were being silly, singing, so I—"

Her words fell silent as Dusty spoke into the phone, then ended the call. "No accident reports," he said. "I'm not sure if that's a good thing or a—"

Charlie opened her mouth to offer a semblance of reassurance to her grandmother but clamped it shut just as quickly. She'd done enough damage.

"Did you hear that?" Sis said, starting for the kitchen.

"Sounds like a car out front," Dusty said, placing the phone on a table.

Charlie ran for the kitchen door, brushing her grandmother aside to jerk it open. She stepped out onto the side porch. "Dad," she called out at the sight of his car.

"Oh, thank God," Sis muttered from behind her.

Charlie didn't wait for the car to stop. She darted the full length of the porch, pushing the screen door with the pad of her palm and leaping over the steps. "Dad!"

Her father exited the automobile as quickly as he could, stepping around his open door. She threw herself fully into his arms, not caring about sliding in the snow, her arms wrapped around his shoulders and her feet leaving the ground. Burying her face into his neck, she whimpered, "Oh, Dad! *Daddy!*" She breathed him in, inhaling the clean scent of snow, the masculine leftovers of his aftershave, and the telltale hint of gasoline. "I'm so sorry."

He enclosed her in his arms. "It's okay, baby." He squeezed tighter. "Whatever it is."

"What's going on?" Marie asked as her car door slammed.

"Where have you been?" Sis called from the doorway before Charlie could answer.

John set his daughter's feet on the snow-covered ground. "The Browers broke down in town." His arm slid easily around Charlie's waist, as hers did around his. "We came up on them and took them home, but then I had trouble with my own car fishtailing on the ice and sliding into an embankment. Had to work her a little to get her back on the road." He threw out his hands. "And I can't find my cell phone."

Marie shrugged. "And I don't have one, I'm afraid."

Sis crossed the distance between the porch steps and her family. "Your phone's in the house." She kissed her son and then Charlie. "You're here now, and that's all that matters." Her misty eyes blinked at Charlie. "We're *all* here now."

"But wait—" Charlie said, stepping away from her father. "I need to know something."

"What's that?" her father asked.

"*Who* is Ivan?"

"Ivan?" Marie asked. "You mean Ivan the Terrible?"

Dusty stood on the top step of the porch and crossed his arms as if bracing himself for the answer.

"Yes," Charlie answered.

John laughed. "That's our name for David Herbick, our landlord. He's one of these it's-the-first-of-the-month-where's-my-check kind of guys." He winced slightly. "Truth is, what with Thanksgiving, we were a little skint this month, and I had to ask him to wait."

Marie leaned against the car and shook her head. "He was none too happy about that. Threatened to shut us down on the phone that morning you were there, Charlie, and then—as you know—he showed up."

"So," Charlie began, her eyes avoiding Dusty altogether, "he's not . . . like a—"

"What?" John asked with a playful smirk. "Like a bookie or a drug dealer or something?"

Charlie looked to her boots, their tops wrapped in snow. "Something like that," she mumbled.

John kissed the top of his daughter's head with a hearty chuckle. "I told you, Charlie. I'm a changed man. Never going back to that life again. And I'm never letting you down again."

Her eyes searched his and saw the sincerity within them. "I believe you. And I'm sorry I doubted."

"Thank you, Charlie. And you're forgiven."

"Just like that?"

"Mm-hmm. Beats years in the penitentiary for exoneration, don't you think?" Then turning to his mother, he said, "Mom, I'm cold. I'm tired. I'm coffee'd out, and I'm about to die for some of your cocoa."

"Well, come on in," Sis said, starting for the steps, Marie and John right behind her. "Marie? Now, if you're a good little elf, I'll share the recipe with you one day."

Charlie waited, watching them head up the steps as Dusty came down, all three chattering at once. By the time he crossed the lawn to where she stood, the side door to the kitchen had rattled shut behind them.

"See," he said, keeping his voice low, "all you had to do was ask."

"I'm an idiot."

"Yeah, but you're a cute idiot." He tugged her braid.

Charlie sighed. "Do you think there's any hope for this girl? You know, to become a little less Ghost of Christmas Past and a little more Ghost of Christmas Present?" She dared not think about the future. Not fully. Not yet.

"It's Christmas, Charlie. There's always hope." He winked. "Come on. Let's get inside before we freeze to death."

Charlie grinned. "I think not, *sur*," she said in her best Oliver Twist accent.

"What do you mean, you 'think not'?" he mimicked her.

She looked up, breathed in the cold air, and smiled at the full moon. Turning, she grabbed Dusty's cold hands in her own and pulled him closer to the tree line where snow lay as thick as a half dozen folded quilts. "Know what I want to do right now?"

He chuckled. "Not *that* again. We're not twelve anymore, Charlie."

"We're not *old* either." Charlie fell back, allowing the snow to catch her, then waved her arms and legs to create a snow angel. "Come on," she said, laughing. "Make one with me!"

He lay beside her, creating his own angel, then rolled over and kissed her. "You're crazy, you know that?"

Her eyes widened. "Crazy in love." She breathed in. Out. "And complete. And happy. And full of life." *Like Scrooge on Christmas Day.* "And—"

"And?"

Charlie threw her arms around Dusty's neck and shouted into the moonlight, "And *God bless us, every one!*"

Group Discussion Guide

1. Charlie loses her job and is forced to move back in with her grandmother. This could seem like an overwhelming loss, but—as Charlie will see—this is God opening a door for her. Can you think of a time when God, without your initial understanding, used the negative for a positive in your life?

2. Charlie has a beautiful memory of going with her parents to cut down a Christmas tree. Do you have any memories like these, either with your parents, your grandparents, or your children?

3. Charlie tends to shy away from "the classics." Why do you think she does?

4. What is your favorite Christmas carol? Why is that one your favorite?

5. Charlie's parents let her down in a significant way when she was a little girl. That disappointment carried on to her adulthood, which made it difficult for her to learn to trust her father, even though he had truly changed. What has God taught you about learning to trust those who have hurt you in the past?

6. Do you have a favorite Christmas ornament? What does it symbolize for you?

7. Charlie volunteers at the homeless shelter her father directs. What do you think she learned about herself and the homeless during that time?

8. What kind of volunteer work have you done? What did you learn from it?

9. Charles Dickens—called "that great Christian writer" by Leo Tolstoy and Fyodor Dostoyevsky—wrote some of the most beloved classics. These include *The Adventures*

of Oliver Twist, David Copperfield, Bleak House, Little Dorrit, A Tale of Two Cities, Great Expectations, and (of course) *A Christmas Carol* (to name a few). Do you have a favorite work of Dickens?

10. Ebenezer Scrooge said, "I will honour Christmas in my heart, and try to keep it all the year. I will live in the Past, the Present, and the Future! The Spirits of all Three shall strive within me. I will not shut out the lessons that they teach." What do you think he meant by that? What does it mean to you?

Want to learn more about Eva Marie Everson
and check out other great fiction from
Abingdon Press?

Check out our website at
www.AbingdonFiction.com
to read interviews with your favorite authors,
find tips for starting a reading group,
and stay posted on what new titles are on the horizon.

Be sure to visit Eva online!

www.evamarieeverson.com

We hope you've enjoyed *God Bless Us Every One*. If you missed Eva Marie Everson's book about Ashlynne and William, we hope you'll check it out. Here's a sample from *The Road to Testament*.

1

Line 4 on my office phone flashed red, letting me know my grandmother, who also happened to be my employer, wanted to speak to me.

"Ashlynne Rothschild," I said, supporting the handset between my ear and shoulder. "Hey, Gram."

"Ashlynne, do you have a minute to come to my office?"

I looked at the piles of work strewed across my desk. For the last hour, my fingers had flown across my computer keyboard in a futile effort to meet a deadline for *Parks & Avenues*, our family's well-heeled local magazine. "Ah . . ."

"I told your father," she said with a tone of confidence, "that we should just wait until this evening over dinner to talk, but he seems to think you need to come to my office now. Come save me, hon."

All right then. Obviously, our meeting was more than a business matter; it was a *family* business matter. "Sure, Gram. Give me ten minutes and I'll be right there." My mouth lifted in a half-grin. "You know, to save you." Though I knew if anyone needed saving, it would be Dad. Constance Rothschild steered this ship, not the other way around.

"Thank you," she whispered before disconnecting the call. I tossed the handset back to its cradle and returned my attention to the computer's monitor. On my desk, a cup of spice tea grew tepid in my Winter Park Arts Festival mug. I took a slow sip, enjoying the flavors and the scent. Looking over the last line I'd written for the cover article I was nearly behind on, I mumbled under my breath: " . . . no more than a footpath leading to . . ."

Fingers poised over the keys, I flexed then typed the conclusion of the sentence.

I hit Control-Save with dramatic flair, as if playing the final notes of a Sergei Rachmaninoff composition. I stood, took a last sip of tea, and left what often felt like a too-small office, but that was—in reality—plenty big.

Courtney Howard-Smith, my young assistant and research guru, worked at her desk, her customary headset firmly in place. I never knew if she listened to music as a muse, if she was doing some sort of research, or just goofing off. In truth, I never asked and she never volunteered. She got her work done and, as the ink still dried on her Rollins diploma, she did it well. She was, like me, a research hound. If I didn't have time to dig, she not only took the assignment, but she often found things I feared I may have missed.

For me, her attention to the most minute of details trumped the issue that Courtney Howard-Smith lived a life completely devoid of revering anyone older than herself by even so much as ten minutes. Or, in my case, ten years. And counting.

I tapped her desk several times with my index finger. She stopped typing, pulled the headset from her head, and laid it to rest around her neck and throat. "Hey there."

"Hey yourself," I said, doing my best to make some sort of personal connection. I smiled, but got nothing short of unblinking eyes in return. "I've got a meeting with my grandmother and, apparently, my father."

"Okay," she said, clearly not impressed. As usual.

I paused to regroup. Once again, when it came to Courtney, there was no connection. I should be used to it by now. Not just with Courtney but with most people. Even though I knew being used to it wouldn't make the pill any easier to swallow. "Do me a favor. Have you seen the photo layout for the new retirement center article?"

"I haven't. No."

"Can you get that for me? I'm not sure why it hasn't been sent yet, and I'm nearly done with the article."

Courtney picked up a pen, jotted a note on a pad of purple paper, and said, "No problem. I'll get to that as soon as I can." She smiled as if the notion to do so had just hit her, then let the smile go.

Unnerving.

I tapped her desk again. My way of saying "good job and goodbye," not that I'm sure it registered. Although I wished it would.

I headed for Gram's office, all the way on the other side of the once one-room warehouse, now sectioned by low cubicle walls. Everything about the room was bright. Cluttered but efficient. Faces of employees focused on computer monitors. Rapidly pecked keys, the musical medley I'd grown up with, echoed around me. This—the desks, the faces, the sound of work—had been a part of my childhood. I'd known, even then, I'd one day be a part of it all. And, all of my life—or so it seemed—I'd dreamed of one day occupying the office with my father's name on the door. And then, one day . . . Gram's.

Yet I knew only a few of the employees by name. And most of those were last names. With the exception of Courtney, they all called me "Miss Rothschild," which suited me just fine. I'd learned a long time ago that the more I protected myself from the intimacies of the personal lives of others, the better off my life would be.

My grandmother's office sat beyond the maze of desks and cubes. I walked purposefully to the glass door etched with CONSTANCE L. ROTHSCHILD across the center, the entrance to a sanctuary barred from view by sheets of glass and white blinds. I tapped, then opened the door without waiting for a response.

Gram sat on the far side of the L-shaped room, beyond a retro bookcase—blond wood, long and low—and behind her sprawling desk, whose size made her diminutive frame seem even more petite. At seventy-eight, she remained in excellent health. She wore her silvery-gray hair in soft curls around her face, brushed back from her forehead, and wore very little makeup. She didn't need to. She was and always had been a natural beauty. An earthiness shone in the sparkling of her blue eyes and the God-given blush of her cheeks.

Her smile welcomed me as I stepped in. "Come in, beautiful child. Come in."

I closed the door behind me. To my left, my father sat on the olive-green sofa in the 1960s-inspired sitting area, one ankle resting casually over a knee, foot bobbing up and down. He talked on his iPhone, "Uh-huh, uh-huh . . . ," then looked over and sent a wink my way.

I smiled at him. He was, like his father—my "Papa"—had been, extraordinarily handsome. "A catch," Gram called him when she teased my mother. "When I gave you my son," she says, "I gave you quite the catch."

And he'd *received* quite the catch, truth be told, and I considered myself *most* fortunate to be their only child.

I didn't know whether to sit with him or amble over to my grandmother. Gram made her way to us, so I lowered myself into one of the boxy, gold-colored chairs and crossed my legs in one movement, a process learned from my mother. Not by instruction, but by observation.

"All right then . . . ," Dad continued. I could tell he was ready to close the conversation. Though I didn't recognize the voice on the other end, the caller clearly wasn't finished speaking.

Gram stood next to me, ran her fingertips along the wide collar of the Kay Unger eyelet suit I wore. "Very pretty," she said.

I smiled at her. In spite of her financial influence and position, Gram rarely wore anything ostentatious. To the office, she typically donned khaki slacks, casual tops, and oversized sweaters. Even in summer. Never at formal gatherings, of course. On those occasions, she slipped into gowns by Veni Infantino or Alberto Makali. Me? I dressed every day as though our mayor might just happen to drop in to say hello. And don't think it hasn't happened. That's just my life.

"Rick," Gram said, "tell Shelton we'll call him again later."

Dad gave his mother a look of appreciation. "Uh . . . yeah. Listen, my daughter just walked in, and both she and Mother are staring at me, so . . ." The voice from the other end rattled off a few more lines. Dad laughed good-naturedly. "All right then. We'll talk about it later . . . thank you again . . . no, seriously. Thank you. Good-bye, sir."

He ended the call, dropped both feet to the floor, hung his head between his shoulders, and rested his elbows on his knees as though he had just run a marathon. "My word that man can talk."

"Talk the ears right off a mule," Gram said. One of her famous sayings she'd picked up while, as she puts it, "living Southern in the earlier years of my marriage." She smiled. "But he is a good egg and a better friend."

Gram sat directly across from me in the matching chair. A maple coffee table stretched between us, its surface scattered with issues of the magazine. Dad leaned back, resting an arm along the sleek line of the sofa. The track lights shining overhead brought a twinkle to eyes the color of a robin's egg. "How ya doing, Kitten?" he asked.

"I'm doing just fine, Dad," I said, suspicion now rising inside me. If the looks they were giving each other—not to mention me—were any indication, something was most definitely up. I looked from him to my grandmother and back again. "What's going on here?"

Gram clapped her hands together. "My darling, your beloved grandmother has decided to retire. Officially and *fully* retire. I see afternoons of nothing but reading and mah-jong in my future."

The air rushed out of my lungs. "Gram . . ." As much as I'd known it would one day happen, I couldn't imagine *Parks & Avenues* or my life without her on a daily basis.

Her face glowed, appearing ten years younger simply having made the announcement. I looked to my father. He swallowed hard, his Adam's apple bobbing up and down in his slender neck. "Dad?"

"It's her decision," he said, leaning over and resting his elbows on his knees. "Don't you think she's earned it?"

I looked around the room. The paneled walls Gram had chosen to complement her '60s-themed décor boasted with award plaques. Framed photographs of Gram with celebrities—local, national, and international—showed her growing older with grace. Not a superstar in New York or Hollywood could compare to her. Joining the plaques and photographs were framed covers of her favorite editions of the magazine.

The only thing hanging that wasn't directly work-related was the massive print over my father's head. A color drawing of a glamorous, curvaceous woman from 1960, gloved hand resting under her chin, hair held back by a Holly Golightly scarf, eyes shielded by Jackie O sunglasses. She leaned back, tilting the full width of the print, from lower right to upper left. The Eiffel Tower stood in abstract white contrast behind her.

Few people knew my grandfather had the print of my grandmother made after one of their trips abroad. "I don't like to brag," she said to me the day I realized the identity of the captivating woman. I was all of thirteen at the time. "But I was quite a beauty, wasn't I?" she asked with a giggle.

Yes. And she still was.

"Wow," I finally said, when nothing else came to mind. "So . . . what does this mean exactly?" Because I could guess . . . and if I were right, all the work, all the laying of the foundation of my career, would finally allow me to reach the first part of my goal.

Dad cleared his throat. "Well now, that's why you're here."

I had thought as much.

"With Mother leaving the magazine, I'll move up to Editorial Director . . ."

My heart hammered in my chest. Oh. My. Goodness. *Finally.*

The promotion I'd worked my little fingers to the bone and my stiletto heels to nubs for. I would take Dad's position as Editor-in-Chief of one of the most prestigious local-color magazines in the entire state of Florida. Perhaps even in the United States.

I sat straight, ready to hear the rest of what my father had to say. But when he said nothing, I looked first at Gram, then back to him. "I assume you are about to tell me I'll take your position?" I tried not to gloat.

Dad's elbows continued to rest on his knees. He cracked his knuckles, an irritating habit both Mother and I typically chastised him for. For now, I chose to stay silent on the subject. "That depends," he said.

"On?"

Gram shifted in her seat. "On how you do."

"Do what?"

"Not do what, dear. Do where."

"Where?"

"So glad you asked. Testament."

"Testament?"

"North Carolina, darling. You'll love it. Start packing."